THE MEN AND WOMEN WITH AN INTEREST IN THE DIABLO GRANT

Judge Earl Stark—Hulking and rough-hewn, haunted by a turbulent past, he has come to Garrison at the behest of the governor of New Mexico Territory. He'll do his damnedest to uphold the law—by his wits if possible, by force if necessary.

Juan Espina—Aged, tattered, and in a perpetual tequila haze, Espina was never suspected of being a descendant of Spanish aristocracy—or the rightful heir to the Diablo Valley. And not many in Garrison are eager to see him claim his legacy.

Don Alfonso Montoya—A suave Mexican diplomat, his poise and courtesy belie his government's fierce interest in the settlement of the Diablo Valley dispute.

Angelina Montoya—Don Alfonso's beautiful daughter won't sit idly by and be pampered. But when she throws herself into the fury of the dispute, she courts great danger as well as her father's disapproval.

Cord Richmond—The hell-raising son of a wealthy Diablo Valley rancher, he stands to lose his inheritance if the Spanish grant is upheld. And he's never lost anything without a fight.

Dolores—A Mexican lady of the evening with secret desires and a tenderness for the drunken Juan Espina—which puzzles her as much as everyone else.

Edmund Wells—Garrison's banker and mayor has done well with the status quo. But when Judge Stark delivers his verdict, this upstanding citizen will not necessarily land on the side of the law.

Books by James M. Reasoner

Stark's Justice
The Hawthorne Legacy
The Diablo Grant

Published by Pocket Books

For orders other than by individual consumers, Pocket Books grants a discount on the purchase of **10 or more** copies of single titles for special markets or premium use. For further details, please write to the Vice-President of Special Markets, Pocket Books, 1230 Avenue of the Americas, New York, NY 10020.

For information on how individual consumers can place orders, please write to Mail Order Department, Paramount Publishing, 200 Old Tappan Road, Old Tappan, NJ 07675.

A JUDGE EARL STARK WESTERN

JAMES M. REASONER

THE DIABLO GRANT

 Producers of **The First Americans,**
The Holts, and **The White Indian.**

Book Creations Inc., Canaan, NY • Lyle Kenyon Engel, Founder

POCKET BOOKS
New York   London   Toronto   Sydney   Tokyo   Singapore

The sale of this book without its cover is unauthorized. If you purchased this book without a cover, you should be aware that it was reported to the publisher as "unsold and destroyed." Neither the author nor the publisher has received payment for the sale of this "stripped book."

This book is a work of fiction. Names, characters, places and incidents are products of the author's imagination or are used fictitiously. Any resemblance to actual events or locales or persons, living or dead, is entirely coincidental.

An *Original* Publication of POCKET BOOKS

POCKET BOOKS, a division of Simon & Schuster Inc.
1230 Avenue of the Americas, New York, NY 10020

Copyright © 1994 by Book Creations Inc.

All rights reserved, including the right to reproduce this book or portions thereof in any form whatsoever. For information address Pocket Books, 1230 Avenue of the Americas, New York, NY 10020

ISBN: 0-671-87142-0

First Pocket Books printing January 1995

10 9 8 7 6 5 4 3 2 1

POCKET and colophon are registered trademarks of Simon & Schuster Inc.

Cover art by Darryl Zudeck

Printed in the U.S.A.

For Tom Johnson and Arthur W. Hackathorn.

THE DIABLO GRANT

Prologue

"Look at this," the old man said in disgust. He picked up the magazine with its untrimmed pages of rough paper and its garishly colored cover. The bold title across the top of the cover read: SIX-SHOOTER TALES.

The little boy sitting on the floor beside the old man's rocking chair looked up. "I like those stories. Daddy reads them to me sometimes."

"He does, eh?" grunted the old man. "Ought to have better taste in his reading material. Look at this story: 'Big Earl and the Diablo Valley Marauders,' by John B. Boothe." He snorted in contempt. "Probably some drunken hack, if you ask me. I bet he keeps a bottle of hooch next to his typewriter and takes a slug or two every time his stories start to make too much sense."

"Big Earl!" the little boy said with a grin. "I like him. I know who he is."

"Pipe down. It'll be a while before your mama and

daddy get back from the picture show, and we got to pass the time somehow. Might as well read some of this tripe." The old man cleared his throat. "'Big Earl knew he had wandered into the desperadoes' trap. "Come on, yuh low-down rannies!" he bellowed as the outlaws charged him. The six-shooters clutched in his hamlike fists belched flaming mayhem as owlhoot lead sang a threnody of death around his ears. The stalwart, fighting frontier jurist ignored his own danger as he returned the gang's fire. He had to save the peaceful settlers of Diablo Valley from the clutches of those evil marauders, even if it cost him his own life.' Phew! What a load of bull!" The old man leaned forward in his chair. "I was in Diablo Valley during all that trouble, you know. I can tell you what *really* happened."

The boy looked up at him and nodded eagerly.

The old man tossed the magazine aside and sat back, clasping his hands together. "Well, you see, it was like this. It all started with this old, old man—"

"Older than you?"

"Huh! I wasn't so old then, let me tell you. Now hush up. Who's telling this story, you or me? Now, like I was saying . . ."

Chapter One

The old man was singing, or trying to, as he stumbled along the street. His voice, cracked and husky from all the years he'd poured raw tequila down his throat, quavered as uncertainly as his gait did. More than once he had to grab at a hitchrack to keep from pitching forward on his face. He was falling-down drunk—a common state of affairs for Juan Espina.

The hour was late in Garrison, New Mexico Territory, and few people were abroad now. Down the street, light spilled past the batwing doors of a saloon. Tinny piano music and the equally tinny laughter of percentage girls drifted out into the night. Around a corner, on a narrow side street, a cantina was still open, and the soft, liquid chords of a guitar floated out from the squat adobe structure. This was where Juan Espina had been drinking until a few minutes earlier. He had spent this evening as he did most evenings: sitting on the floor in a corner with his knees drawn up in front of him, a bottle cradled in his hands, his dark, rheumy eyes watching with half-remembered desire as young women in low-cut blouses flirted with drunken cowboys and eventually led them out to the little shacks behind the cantina. Juan recalled what men and women did there, but the tequila had long since reduced his interest in it to a feeling of dim nostalgia. He was content to sit and smile lazily as he took an occasional healthy swallow from the bottle.

Not too much, a small voice in the back of his brain had warned him, as it always did. His coins were few, and the bottle had to last the evening.

That was all right with Juan. He thought sometimes that he never really sobered up, and one bottle a night was enough to keep the fires within him stoked. That was precisely as he wanted it; that way he recalled only the good things, not the bad.

Now he was on his way home, making his way unsteadily toward the edge of the settlement to the hovel that was his only because no one else in Garrison was willing to live in such squalor. Not even the whores would deign to stay in such a place. But that was all right with Juan, too. At least no one bothered him there. It was a haven of sorts, because he had enemies. Oh, yes. Even a *viejo* such as he had enemies.

He staggered, caught the hitchrack again, and held himself up for a long moment until the spinning that gripped his head eased slightly. When he felt steady enough to move on again, he let go of the rail, took a tentative step forward, and fell. He grunted loudly as he hit the ground, more surprised than hurt.

The Diablo Grant

In the mouth of a nearby alley, two figures moved in the darkness. One of them, a man, was grunting like a pig. Over that noise, his companion heard the sound of the old drunk's collapse and looked over his shoulder to see the sticklike figure in ragged cotton pants and tunic lying at the edge of the street. She hissed, *"Alto!"* and pushed her hands against the chest of the cowboy who had her pinned against the wall of a building.

"Huh?" the cowboy asked. "What the hell you mean, stop? I just got started good, honey."

"Let me go," the young woman said.

"I done gave you the money," the cowboy said, his voice turning ugly and resentful. "And I ain't finished yet, so you just hold still. You want to go to squirmin' around, put that in what you're 'sposed to be doin'."

"You do not understand—"

"The hell I don't."

The young woman closed her eyes, clenched her teeth, and tried not to worry too much about the old man as the cowboy began moving again. Surely old Juan was all right, she told herself. It was said that God watched over fools and drunkards, and Juan Espina was surely both those things. It would be faster to let the cowboy finish with her than to argue with him.

As she expected, that did not take long. When he was done, the cowboy tried to give her a sloppy kiss and stick his tongue in her mouth, but she turned her head away. He had not paid for *that*. Muttering and breathing heavily, the cowboy buttoned up his pants and stumbled away down the alley. He had been drinking quite a bit himself, although he was nowhere near as far gone as Juan.

5

The woman rearranged her skirts and hurried out of the alley, going over to kneel next to the old man. "Juan," she said as she put her hand on his shoulder. "Juan, you must get up."

His breath was rasping in his throat. He shifted enough to twist his neck and peer up at her in confusion. He mumbled a name. "Antonia?"

"No, it is Dolores. Come, Juan. We must get you home."

She did not know who Antonia was—or who Antonia had *been,* more likely. Perhaps she had been married to Juan sometime in the dim past. But if so it had been long, long ago, because Dolores had known the old man ever since she was a little girl, and as far back as she could remember, he had been alone. Alone except for his tequila.

"Ah, Dolores, *muchacha.* As always, you come to the rescue of this old fool."

"Someone has to," Dolores said, trying not to sound bitter. She reminded herself that she had no one to blame for this burden. She had appointed herself the old man's guardian angel.

Some angel, she thought. Juan had no one to look after him except a *puta,* a whore who sold herself to any cowboy who had the coins. But that was better than nothing, she supposed.

Carefully she helped him to his feet. Old bones were brittle, and there was not much left of Juan except bones. He was as gaunt as a starved dog. He ate only occasionally, Dolores knew, not from lack of money for food but from sheer lack of interest in anything but the bottle he nursed each night in the cantina. Juan was a poor man, true, but he usually had enough coins

The Diablo Grant

for some beans and tortillas in addition to the liquor, if only he could trouble himself to buy them and eat.

She would see that he got some food tomorrow, Dolores promised herself, even if she had to force him to eat.

When he was standing up again, she cautiously let go of him and reached down to pick up the battered sombrero that had fallen off. She smoothed down the wild strands of snow-white hair and settled the hat on his head. In the moonlight she could make out the gaunt cheeks and the silver-stubbled jaw. He wheezed loudly as she draped his left arm around her shoulders and put her right arm around his waist to support him. Awkwardly—he was considerably taller than she—they started down the street.

"Wait a minute," someone said from the boardwalk. "Let me give you a hand."

Dolores looked up to see a man standing in front of a door and locking it. He had apparently just come out of the building, which was dark now. Although she had never really learned to read, she knew the gilt-lettered writing on the front window said GARRISON TERRITORIAL OBSERVER. It was the name of the local newspaper, and as the man emerged from the shadows of the boardwalk into the moonlight that flooded the street, she recognized him as Matthew Curry, the young editor of the paper.

She had seen Curry around town many times in the year since he had come to Garrison to take over the failing newspaper. He was very handsome, she thought, with his broad shoulders, dark hair, and quick, friendly smile. She would not have minded if he had come to her and paid for her favors, would not have minded at all. But of course he had never even glanced at her, as far as she could tell. Why should he? A young, handsome *Americano* journalist would have no use for a Mexican whore. Matthew Curry undoubtedly had his choice of respectable young women in Garrison, although, Dolores thought smugly, she could show him many things that would shock those icy-blooded señoritas but would pleasure him greatly.

At the moment, however, all she was interested in was getting Juan Espina safely back to his shack. If he passed out in the street again, he might be run over in the darkness by a wagon or a careless rider. She did not want the old man's death on her hands.

"If you would help me, señor," she said to Curry, "I would greatly appreciate it."

"What's wrong with the old man?" Curry asked as he stepped up to them and put his left arm around Juan. "Is he sick?"

Dolores did not want to lie to him. "No, he—"

Curry sniffed and said with a chuckle, "Never mind. I reckon I can tell what his problem is. Tequila."

Dolores felt a quick flash of resentment. "He is old and has no family. He has nothing else."

"Hold on," Curry said as he helped her steer Juan down the street. He was supporting most of the old man's weight now, such as it was. "I didn't mean anything by it. I recognize Juan now."

Of course he did. Juan Espina was the—what did the *Americanos* call it? Town drunk? That was it. Juan Espina was the town drunk, and everyone in Garrison knew him. Some pitied him, some reviled him, some found him only a source of amusement. But everyone seemed to know him.

"I am taking him to his house so that he can sleep," Dolores told Curry. "I am grateful for your help."

"Sure," he said easily. "I was just locking up for the night when I saw the two of you going by. What's your name?"

She hesitated, then said, "Dolores."

"Pretty name," he commented. "I'm Matt Curry."

"I know," she said without thinking, then caught her lower lip between her teeth.

Curry didn't seem to think anything of it. "Doesn't weigh much, does he?" he said. "A little hard to handle, though. He's so long and lanky."

"I have taken him home many times."

"Oh?"

Again Dolores's teeth clenched. She had not meant that the way it sounded. She took pity on old Juan, that was all. True, she was a little surprised that he had never made any advances toward her, even at his age and in his generally drunken condition. She thought of all the times she had lowered Juan onto his dilapidated cot, leaning over him so that her heavy breasts dangled practically out of the low-cut blouse and in his face. Most men in the same position, even if they had been on their deathbed, would have reached up to fondle her, she knew. In fact, one time she had tried to slip her fingers into Juan's pants, thinking to give the pitiful old-timer a moment's pleasure, but he had caught her wrist and forced her hand away with surprising strength and vehemence, insisting that she leave him.

But she could not explain all this to Matthew Curry. It would have been much too embarrassing, and even a whore could feel shame. Instead she kept her mouth shut and moved on down the street with the old man stumbling along beside her, the *Americano* on the other side helping to hold him up.

Matt Curry wasn't sure why he had been so quick to volunteer. A drunken old man and a soiled dove—hardly the kind of folks a rising young newspaper editor should concern himself with. But it was night, and there weren't many people out and about at this hour. He could lend them a hand without anybody's having to know about it.

Matt's face flushed at that thought. He *ought* to be ashamed of himself. His father hadn't raised him to look down on folks, no matter who or what they were.

But old Edward Farrington Curry, publisher of successful newspapers in Baltimore, Philadelphia, and Boston, would have been shocked to see what his son was doing right now, Matt thought with a grin. Despite his democratic ideals, the old boy could be a bit of a stuffed shirt sometimes.

Sensing that Dolores was upset about something, Matt thought about what she had told him and went on, "I'd say old Juan's a lucky man to have somebody like you looking out for him, Dolores."

She shook her head. "He is not lucky. There must have been some very bad thing in his life to make him the way he is."

"Well, could be," Matt agreed. "But I reckon it could be worse. At least somebody cares enough about him to get him out of the street."

"*Sí*. I do not want him to be hurt any worse than he already is."

Juan's head had been hanging forward loosely, but

The Diablo Grant

now he raised it suddenly and called, "Antonia! *Donde estás*, Antonia?"

"Who's that he's asking for?"

Dolores shook her head again. "I do not know. Someone from his past. Whoever she was, she is probably . . . gone."

Matt guessed from the hesitation that Dolores had been about to say "dead," then changed her mind, not wanting to upset Juan. He would be easier to handle if he stayed calm.

Juan's anxiety seemed to subside, and he hung his head again and mumbled incoherently as they guided him along the street. After a few minutes Dolores turned onto a side street and nodded toward the shack that stood at the end of it. "He lives there."

Matt peered at the small structure. It was leaning perilously to one side, and in the moonlight he could see gaping holes in its walls. It might offer a little protection from the elements, but not much. Still, it was better than nothing, and Matt supposed Juan didn't really care what the place looked like. A reasonably solid roof over his head was all that would matter to the old man.

"Let's get him inside," Matt said. "Watch out for snakes in there."

"I know. I have brought him to this place many times. There is a candle inside."

Matt reached inside his coat with his free hand. He brought out a small tin box of matches and held it out to Dolores. "You go first and light the candle," he told her. "I can hold on to Juan."

She hesitated a moment, then took the matches, being careful not to touch his fingers with hers. She was trying to be considerate, Matt knew; she probably figured he wouldn't want to touch somebody like her, even by accident.

While he held Juan upright, Dolores scratched a lucifer against the rough strip on the side of the box and went into the cabin, looking around first to make sure no rattlers had crawled in. The light turned into a flickering yellow glow as she lit the candle.

Matt said, "Let's go, old-timer," as he gently prodded Juan through the sagging, narrow doorway.

Inside, he gazed around the single room, taking in all there was to see—which wasn't much. A bunk made of rope stretched over a crude frame sat against the right-hand wall. To the left was an old, scarred, low table with only three legs; a rock had been dragged in from outside to prop up the fourth corner, but the table still leaned crazily. Against the back wall was a small leather trunk, cracked and ancient looking. Several empty tequila bottles lay on the hard-packed earthen floor. Dried, curled-up tortilla husks crunched under Matt's feet as he led Juan over to the bunk. There was no mattress and only a thin gray blanket, but the night was warm and that would be sufficient.

Carefully Matt lowered Juan onto the bunk while Dolores stood by, holding the candle. The old man fell back limply on the blanket. Matt picked up his feet and legs and put them on the bunk as well. Juan's eyes were closed, and he immediately rolled onto his side and began to snore loudly. It was an ugly, liquid sound.

Dolores handed the candle to Matt. "Hold this, *por favor*," she said. "I want to cover him. He is an old man and chills easily."

"Sure," Matt said. He stood back and let Dolores

The Diablo Grant

work a fold of the blanket loose so that she could drape it over Juan's slumbering form.

In idle curiosity Matt looked around the room again. Something under the leaning table caught his eye, and he bent down and grasped the thick, rectangular object he had spotted there. It was a book, he realized, and the idea that someone like Juan would own one made him even more curious.

The book was covered with a thick layer of dust, and it had gotten wet at some time in the past; the edges of the pages were warped and stained. Matt set it on the table, where it slid a couple of inches before stopping, and brushed off some of the dust. The book was bound in leather, which was something of a surprise. He wiped away more dust and saw that words were embossed in the leather—Spanish words. He knew the language well enough to realize that he was looking at a Bible.

"What are you doing?" Dolores asked sharply.

"Looking at this old Bible," Matt replied. "You reckon it belongs to Juan?"

"I have seen him hold it sometimes, although not for many months. I am sure it is his. You should not disturb it."

"I'm not disturbing it," Matt said as he opened the thick volume. "I'm just looking at it."

He glanced at Dolores and saw that she was watching him with her arms folded across her ample bosom and her full lips pressed tightly together in disapproval. He couldn't blame her, he supposed. Old Juan didn't have much to his name, that was for sure, but certainly other people had no right to tamper with what he did have. Matt was about to replace the book under the table, but first he riffled the pages to see if anything was tucked inside. He had a natural love of books, books of any kind, and it was difficult not to examine one when he came across it.

Several sheets of parchment slipped from among the pages.

Matt frowned, thinking at first that some pages had come loose from the binding. Then he saw that the sheets were not part of the Bible at all, but rather some sort of document that had been pressed inside. They were folded together, and there was a seal on one of them that looked vaguely familiar.

"Here," he said suddenly, thrusting the candle back into Dolores's hands. She was so startled that she took it. "I want to take a closer look at these papers."

"Those are not yours," she protested. "They belong to Juan—"

"I know. I'm not going to do anything to them. I just want to see if I can figure out what they are." He knew this was none of his business, but his journalist's instincts had gotten hold of him now. He wanted to know the facts.

He unfolded the sheets of parchment. As he had suspected, they were covered with fine, spidery writing in faded ink. Elaborate curlicues adorned the words, making them harder to decipher, and the first sheet was decorated with several drawings, including a reproduction of the same seal that embellished the outer page of the documents.

The writing was in Spanish; no surprise there, either. Matt's frown deepened as he tried to translate what he was reading. "You may have to help me with this," he said to Dolores. "My border lingo's not bad,

The Diablo Grant

but I have a little trouble reading all this fancy stuff."

"I . . . I cannot read," she said, sounding mortified. He looked up quickly, saw the shame on her face, and wished he hadn't said anything.

"That's all right," he told her. "I can make out some of it. In fact—" He stiffened abruptly and exclaimed, "Good Lord!"

"What is it?" she asked anxiously. "What have you found?"

He looked up, his eyes wide and his pulse hammering. "I'm not sure, but I think this is a land grant. A royal land grant from the king of Spain, and it's well over a hundred years old."

Dolores shook her head in confusion. "I do not understand. What does the king of Spain have to do with New Mexico?"

She wouldn't understand, Matt realized. She had never been to school, never studied history. In all likelihood her world didn't extend much beyond Garrison's borders.

"Spain owned all this land a long time ago," he explained, "before Mexico became an independent country. Then the United States wound up with the territory after the Mexican War, nearly forty years ago."

"I have heard a little talk about this, but I have never understood it."

"Here's what's important," Matt went on, his excitement growing as he continued to study the documents in his hands. "When Spain still owned all of this part of the country, the king gave sections of it to friends of his. You know, political allies, military leaders, and such. He granted them the land to own forever."

"He could do this thing?" Dolores asked.

15

"Sure. He was the king—he could do pretty much what he wanted." Matt tapped the sheets of parchment and went on, his voice shaking a little. "And this is one of those land grants, covering the entire Diablo Valley. The valley's just about the best ranching country in the whole territory."

Dolores nodded impatiently. "I still do not understand. Why would Juan have this . . . this land grant?"

"Because the king of Spain gave the whole valley to somebody named Emiliano Espina, to belong to him and his heirs forever, in perpetuity." Matt's finger stabbed at the documents again. "That's what it says right here, as best I can make out."

"Emiliano . . . *Espina*?" repeated Dolores, wonder edging into her voice. She stared at the old man sleeping on the rope bunk. "But Juan's name is Espina."

"I know," Matt said hollowly. "This is an old family Bible, and I reckon it means Juan is a descendant of Emiliano Espina."

"But that would mean—" Dolores broke off in shock as she lifted a hand to her mouth.

"Yep," Matt said. "If this is true, it means that Juan Espina really owns the whole dad-blamed Diablo Valley."

On the bunk, Juan rolled over again, broke wind loudly, and resumed snoring.

Chapter Two

It took a long time to get the old man awake again. Getting him sober as well was too much to hope for, Matt decided. He would simply have to try to make Juan understand what he was talking about.

"Is this your Bible, Juan?" he asked, holding out the dusty, leather-bound book.

Juan was sitting up on the bunk, grasping his head in gnarled, age-spotted hands. After blinking several times and trying to focus, he stared at the Bible and nodded slowly. *"Sí,"* he said. *"La Biblia de mi familia*, given to me by *mi madre*. Why do you have it?"

"I found it under the table," Matt said. "You've had it a long time, haven't you?"

"Sí. It is old, very old. From the time when . . . when this land belonged to Spain."

Matt's pulse began to pound again. Juan seemed to

have a firm enough grasp on reality at the moment to understand what Matt was going to ask him next.

"I found these papers in the Bible," he said, laying aside the book and picking up the documents. He glanced at Dolores, who had set the candle carefully on the leaning table and was now watching intently as he questioned the old man. Turning his attention back to Juan, he went on, "Do you recognize them?"

Juan reached out with a trembling hand. Matt hesitated, for some reason reluctant to give the documents to him. But they *did* belong to Juan, after all. Matt handed them over, and they crackled as Juan looked through them.

"Oh, *sí*," Juan said after a long moment. "The old land grant. I had almost forgotten it was in the Bible."

"Then you know what it is?" Matt exclaimed.

Juan waved a quivering hand. "Of course. It is a worthless piece of paper." He was about to throw the documents on the floor when Matt caught his wrist.

"Wait!" the young man cried. "These papers are important!"

"No," Juan said, shaking his head. "They mean nothing. This is not Spain. This is the United States now. The papers are no good."

"You're wrong, Juan. When Mexico achieved its independence from Spain, the old land grants were left intact. And when the treaty was signed ending the war between the United States and Mexico back in the forties, it was agreed that most of the land grants in territory acquired from Mexico would be honored. Don't you see what this means, Juan? You own the Diablo Valley, every bit of it!"

The Diablo Grant

The old man's bleary eyes widened until it seemed they would pop out of his head. "No," he whispered, then said it again louder. "No! I own nothing!"

Holding her hand out, Dolores stepped forward, as if she wanted to prevent Matt from upsetting Juan further. Matt motioned sharply to stop her, caught up in his own excitement at the story he had accidentally uncovered. "Do you have any brothers and sisters, aunts and uncles, cousins?" he asked Juan.

The old man shook his head. "No. I am alone."

"And this Emiliano Espina was one of your ancestors?"

"*Sí*. My great-great-great-grandfather. But that does not make me—"

"Yes, it does," Matt insisted. "This may well be one of the grants that the Treaty of Guadalupe Hidalgo allowed to stand. The only way for you to find out is to open legal proceedings and claim ownership of the Diablo Valley."

Juan stared at the young editor in amazement. "I could not do such a thing."

"Sure you could. You've got to."

Juan shook his head and trembled. "I could not . . . I could not."

Matt took the land grant papers from him and placed them on the table with the Bible. Then he gripped Juan's shoulders and said, "I'll help you. I promise we'll find out the truth, Juan."

Dolores spoke up suddenly. "And what do you get in return for your help, Señor Curry?"

He looked at her, feeling a surge of anger that he quickly suppressed. Naturally someone from her background would think first of the profit angle. He said, "I just want Juan to get what's coming to him, Dolores. That's all."

And a good story, he added to himself. One hell of a story, in fact. This might even get picked up by the papers back east. Then his father could no longer claim that Matt had gone west to bury himself in a place where nobody would see him fail. No more sighs of disappointment or comments about Matt's not being able to succeed in the cutthroat competition of big-city newspapers back east. Edward Farrington Curry would finally see that his son was a damned good newspaperman.

"You do not know what you are doing," Dolores said. "The old man wants only his tequila and a place to sleep."

Juan looked up, his seamed face brightening at the mention of tequila. Matt ignored the pleading in his eyes and said, "Juan can buy all the tequila he'd ever want pretty soon. He's going to be a rich man, a very rich man."

"I . . . I do not know." Juan's thin voice quavered.

Matt's hand tightened on the bony old shoulder. "Trust me," he said. "This is going to turn the whole valley on its ear."

"Son of a bitch!"

Travis Richmond slammed the folded newspaper down on the desk in his study, knocking some of the papers littering the desk onto the floor. Richmond had been trying to catch up on his book work—the worst damned part of being a rancher, he had muttered to himself probably a thousand times during his years of

The Diablo Grant

raising cattle—when his son Cord had come into the study and tossed the newspaper in front of him with a casual, "Thought you'd better take a look at that. I picked it up in town this morning."

Now Cord was across the room, pouring himself a drink. Richmond looked around and said sharply, "Don't you get enough of that in Garrison?"

Cord tossed the whiskey down his throat and wiped the back of his other hand across his mouth. "What do you keep the stuff here for if you don't want anybody to drink it?"

Richmond glared at his son. Cord was a grown man, but he sure as hell didn't act like it sometimes.

There was some family resemblance between the two, but not much. Cord had always taken after his mama, which Richmond supposed was one reason he had never taken a hard enough line with the boy while Cord was growing up. Richmond was tall and lean, with hawklike features burned to the color of saddle leather by the New Mexico sun. His hair was iron-gray, and so was the mustache under his prominent blade of a nose. He wore range clothes, even when he knew he was going to be inside the ranch house all day wrestling with numbers in ledger books. He had threatened plenty of times to hire a blamed pencil-pusher to take care of that, but he couldn't bring himself to trust anybody else. Not when it came to running the spread he'd spent decades building up.

Cord was tall, too, but heavier, broader across the shoulders and face. He had a thick shock of blond hair, and women seemed to think he was handsome. Lord knew there were enough of them flocking around him every time he went to a dance in town, his father thought. Cord's denim pants, work shirt, and black-and-white cowhide vest were functional enough, but a band of silver conchos circled the black Stetson he wore, and the big Spanish rowels on his spurs were equally flamboyant. Richmond had long since given up trying to convince him not to dress like a dandy.

The worst part of it was the ivory-handled Colt riding in the holster that was slung low on Cord's right hip. It was a shootist's gun, and Richmond was afraid that was the way Cord fancied himself. No good would come of it; Travis Richmond was sure of that.

But at the moment he had other, more pressing worries. He prodded the newspaper headline with a blunt fingertip and asked, "You reckon there's anything to this?"

"Don't know, but everybody in town's sure as hell talking about it," Cord replied with a shrug of his wide shoulders.

The headline read: LAND GRANT REVEALS NEW OWNER OF DIABLO VALLEY. That was shocking enough in itself, but a quick reading of the story had told Richmond that things were even worse. It seemed that an elderly Mexican, one Juan Espina, had been discovered to be in possession of a royal grant from the king of Spain that gave his family ownership of the entire valley. As the only survivor of the family, Espina was claiming the whole shooting match for himself. It was the most ridiculous thing Richmond had ever read.

He said as much with a snort of disgust. "I've owned this ranch for nigh onto thirty years. I'll be damned if I'm going to let some raggedy-ass Mexican get away with saying it's his!"

The Diablo Grant

"It's not just Antlers," Cord said. "This Espina fella says *everything* is his. Our spread, and Ben Tompkins's place, and the whole blasted town of Garrison, as well as all the smaller farms and ranches." Cord poured himself another drink. "I've seen Espina around. He's nothing but a drunk."

"You'd certainly know him, then," Richmond said, goading his son out of habit more than anything else.

Cord flushed but otherwise ignored the jibe. "You're right. We can't let him get away with it."

Richmond picked up the *Territorial Observer* and read on. "Says here that damned Texas lawyer Billy Chadwick is representing him. Leave it to a Texan to make a mess of everything. He ought to go back to Pecos where he came from!"

"I hear Chadwick's wired Santa Fe with the old man's claim. Reckon it'll all have to be hashed out in court." Cord sipped from his whiskey, then went on slowly, "Unless that Mexican could be persuaded to drop his claim."

Richmond glanced sharply at him. "What do you mean by that?"

Before Cord could answer, the sound of hoofbeats came from outside, and Richmond turned to look out the open window. Several riders were trotting into view. He cursed.

"It's Tompkins," he said. "What the hell's he doing here?"

Without waiting for Cord to speculate on the answer, Richmond stalked out of the study and down the hall to the foyer. Cord followed, and he wasn't far behind when Richmond stepped out onto the gallery that ran along the front of the big, whitewashed house. Out of habit the younger man's hand hovered near the butt of his ivory-handled Colt, in case there was trouble.

There usually was when Travis Richmond and Ben Tompkins went to butting heads.

Two of Tompkins's hands from the Box BT were with the barrel-chested cattleman. Like all of Tompkins's crew, they looked more like gunslingers than cowboys to Richmond. The whole bunch was bad news as far as he was concerned. Probably wide-loopers, the lot of them—just like their boss.

"Howdy, Travis," Tompkins said with exaggerated cordiality as he reined in and cuffed back his hat from over his heavy, florid features. He rested his hands on the saddlehorn and leaned forward. Richmond didn't invite him to get down from his horse, and that seemed to come as no surprise to Tompkins. "How you doin'?"

"You didn't ride over here to ask about my health, Ben," Richmond snapped. "Whatever brings you here, spit it out."

Tompkins chuckled. "You never was one for beatin' around the bush, was you, Travis?" He reached into one of his saddlebags and brought out a folded newspaper. "You seen this?"

"If it's this week's *Observer*, I have. You're talking about the story about that old Mexican." Richmond's clipped words were a statement, not a question.

"Damn right I am! You ever heard such a load of buffalo droppin's in your life? The whole idea of a damn Meskin ownin' this valley just don't make sense!"

"According to the newspaper, he has one of those old Spanish land grants. A lot of them have been upheld by the courts." Richmond still thought the situa-

The Diablo Grant

tion was as ludicrous as Tompkins obviously did, but he found himself naturally playing the devil's advocate. The two ranchers had been rivals for a long time. More than rivals, really—"enemies" was probably a more accurate description. There had never been a shortage of bad blood between them.

Tompkins said, "Nobody's takin' my ranch away from me, specially not some ol' Meskin drunk. Why, Espina probably ain't been sober a day in the past twenty years! What'n hell's he goin' to do with the whole Diablo Valley?"

"He'll never get his hands on it," Richmond declared. "No court in the land would honor such a farfetched claim."

Tompkins narrowed his eyes. "You willin' to bet Antlers on that, Travis? Because that's what you'll be doin'."

"Well, what do you suggest?" Richmond demanded impatiently.

Without being asked, Ben Tompkins swung down from his saddle and handed the reins to one of his men. He stepped up onto the gallery and faced Richmond squarely. Cord edged forward, tensing and moving his hand closer to his gun. Tompkins's men did likewise. More than one face-to-face confrontation like this between Travis Richmond and Ben Tompkins had ended in a fight.

That apparently wasn't what Richmond wanted this time. He motioned Cord back and prodded Tompkins. "Well?"

"We got to fight this thing," Tompkins said. "We've had our problems in the past, but we got to work together this time, Travis. 'Tween you and me, we own most of Diablo Valley. We stand to lose the most if that Meskin gets his hands on it legal-like. So we got to stop him."

"That's what I was saying, Pa," growled Cord.

"Hush up, boy," Richmond said. He studied Tompkins shrewdly and went on, "Are you talking about fighting this in court?"

"Way I see it, we got to. We homesteaded our spreads fair and square, built 'em up by buyin' out other folks, did everything just the way we was supposed to. Did it in good faith, too."

Richmond wasn't so sure about that where Tompkins was concerned. Back in the days when Tompkins was expanding the Box BT, rumors had spread about barns burning down, wells being poisoned, and bulls being shot. Some of the smaller ranchers who wouldn't entertain legitimate offers from Richmond had sold out to Tompkins. A couple of men had even wound up dead, shot from ambush, and their families had sold their land to Tompkins right after that. Nobody had ever been able to prove anything against the man, though, and anyway, there was a bigger concern facing them now. Tompkins was right about one thing: There was never any way of knowing what a court would do. If Espina's claim was allowed to proceed unopposed . . .

"All right," Richmond said abruptly, scarcely believing the words coming out of his own mouth, "we'll work together on this, Ben. We'll bring in a lawyer from Santa Fe, somebody who'll make short work of Billy Chadwick."

Tompkins nodded emphatically. "Damn right. We'll get the whole thing thrown out of court." He stuck out a hand.

Richmond hesitated only briefly, then gripped the

The Diablo Grant

other man's hand and shook it. It was a dark day, he thought, when he had to cooperate with Ben Tompkins, but the situation called for desperate measures.

Cord evidently thought so, too. When Tompkins had mounted up again and ridden off with his men, the younger Richmond said, "I never thought I'd see anything like that."

"Neither did I," grunted his father. "But Tompkins and I have to put a stop to this before it goes too far."

"Yeah, but what if that lawyer the two of you bring in doesn't do any good?"

Richmond looked at his son. "We'll deal with that problem when it happens, not before."

Cord laughed humorlessly. "What was that you used to tell me? Cut off a rattlesnake's head when it's little, so it can't grow up to bite you? Seems like this snake's already pretty big, Pa. Better not waste any time cutting its head off."

With a sardonic grin he stepped down off the gallery and sauntered toward the bunkhouse. Richmond supposed he was going off to play poker with some of the hands. That seemed to be one of Cord's favorite pastimes, after getting drunk and bedding saloon girls.

Richmond sighed and went back into the house. For all his failings, Cord was right about one thing: The rattlesnake threatening them—Juan Espina's claim to the Diablo Valley—was looking mighty damned big right about now, and there was venom dripping from the fangs in its open mouth.

Matt Curry heard his name being called and turned around. The man coming quickly toward him on the boardwalk was Billy Chadwick.

The attorney was several inches shorter than Matt,

but he had an air of compact power about him. He was wearing a dark suit, a white shirt, a black string tie, and a cream-colored Stetson over graying, sandy hair. A gun belt was strapped around his waist, and a Colt with well-worn walnut grips rode in the holster under his coat.

Matt knew that Chadwick had moved to Garrison a few years earlier after spending most of his life in Texas. He had heard that Chadwick had been a partner in a successful law practice in Pecos, but when the younger half of the team had quit the law to go into ranching, Chadwick's natural restlessness had led him to New Mexico Territory. He didn't talk much about himself, but there were rumors that he had been an Indian fighter and perhaps even a Texas Ranger in his youth. Chadwick was a canny lawyer; he had won most of his cases since coming to Garrison.

"What can I do for you, Mr. Chadwick?" Matt asked as the attorney came up to him. It was early evening, and Matt had closed the office of the *Observer* a short while before. He was on his way to the hotel to eat supper in the dining room.

Chadwick had a copy of the newspaper in his hand, and he brandished it as he said, "I'd like to know what the hell you thought you were doing by printing this."

The lawyer's sharp, angry tone took Matt by surprise. He frowned and said, "Why, I was just doing my job. I *am* the editor of the paper, you know."

"When you brought Señor Espina to see me yesterday and showed me those land grant documents, I agreed to take his case," Chadwick said. "I didn't say it was all right for you to plaster it all over the paper."

The Diablo Grant

"What was I supposed to do? It's a great story!" Matt felt a surge of resentment. "I would think you'd be pleased, Mr. Chadwick. This case is going to put you on the map!"

"I've *been* on the map," Chadwick replied dryly. "I came to Garrison because I thought it would be a nice, quiet place to live and practice a little law. But you're going to have this whole part of the territory in an uproar by playing up the story like this." He slapped the newspaper.

Matt shrugged. "I thought I was doing the right thing."

"Well, now everybody who might oppose Señor Espina's claim has been warned about what's going to happen. Men like Travis Richmond and Ben Tompkins are going to be mad as hell when they read this. As far as they're concerned, Diablo Valley belongs to *them*."

"They're wrong about that," Matt snapped. "They might as well find it out now as later."

Chadwick looked at him for a long moment, then sighed and shook his head. "Where's Juan Espina now?" he asked.

Matt frowned. "How should I know? I haven't seen him since we went to your office yesterday."

"Damn it, boy, somebody ought to be keeping an eye on him. Come on."

Chadwick took off down the sidewalk, striding so fast that Matt had to hurry to keep up with him despite his longer legs. He resented Chadwick's talking to him like that, but he didn't figure the older man was in any mood to hear him complain. Chadwick was mad enough at him already—although Matt still couldn't understand -what he was so het up about. The case would just have to run its course through the courts. What else could happen?

"Where does Espina live?" Chadwick called over his shoulder.

"Right up here," Matt replied. "Turn there at the corner, and his shack is down at the end of the street—"

That was when Matt heard the shouting and then, a second later, the flat boom of a gunshot.

Chadwick threw a startled glance at Matt, then broke into a run. Matt was right behind him as they rounded the corner. The yelling and the shot had come from the direction of Juan's shack. Matt saw three horses standing in front of it, their reins dangling. The daylight was fading, but as the two men hurried past the animals, Matt saw the Antlers brand—a stylized pattern representing the antlers on a buck deer—burned into the horses' flanks.

Antlers was Travis Richmond's spread, and Richmond was one of the two largest landholders in Diablo Valley. He stood to lose a great deal if Juan's claim was upheld in court.

That thought flashed through Matt's mind, but there was no time for more speculation. He could still hear angry shouts, louder now, from inside the shack. Someone yelled, "Give it up, old man!"

Chadwick had his hand on the butt of his gun as he ducked through the open door. Matt entered the shack a second later and saw three men clustered around a pathetic figure on the floor. Juan was trying to scuttle away from the men surrounding him. One of them—in the dim light, Matt thought he recognized Cord Rich-

The Diablo Grant

mond, the rancher's son—had a pistol in his hand and was brandishing it as he threatened the old man.

With a whisper of steel against leather, Chadwick drew his Colt and leveled it at the interlopers. "Drop that gun, damn it!" he grated. "I mean it, Cord!"

The cowboy holding the revolver looked up at the newcomers. It was indeed Cord Richmond, and his face was set in harsh, ugly lines. "You'd better get out of here, Chadwick," Cord said. "This ain't none of your business."

"The hell it's not. Juan Espina is my client, and I'm not going to let you hurt him."

"I'm not hurting him," Cord shot back. "I'm just trying to talk some sense into his foolish old head."

"Trying to get that land grant away from him, that's what you mean," Chadwick accused.

"Well, what the hell's he going to do with the Diablo Valley? Are you saying my pa and Ben Tompkins ought to just turn their ranches over to this piss-ant Mexican after working years and years to build them up?"

"I'm saying it's not going to do your case any good when the judge hears about how you tried to bully Juan into giving up his claim. And for your information, Cord, the land grant document isn't here. It's where you can't get your hands on it and destroy it."

Matt could tell from the way Cord Richmond's face twisted that that was exactly what he'd had in mind. Without the old papers, Juan had no case at all.

Cord glanced over Chadwick's shoulders, his gaze resting on Matt for a moment. Then he said to the lawyer, "There's just one of you and three of us, Chadwick. Maybe you're the one who'd better stop waving a gun around. You can't count on any help from that Yankee paper-pusher."

Matt knew he ought to speak up. Despite the fact that the guns made him decidedly nervous, he began, "You don't scare us, Richmond—"

"I'll handle this, Matt," Chadwick cut in. He smiled thinly at Cord and said, "You're right. I reckon your boys could both throw down on me at the same time, and I wouldn't have a chance. But you'd die before I did, Cord."

Even in the gathering shadows Matt could see Cord's face go pale and the gun in his hand tremble a little. "You'll be sorry for this, Chadwick," Cord finally said as he holstered the weapon. "My pa's lawyer will cut you up into little pieces, and that old drunk won't be any better off than when you started all this."

"I'll take my chances in court," Chadwick said coolly. "Now take your men and get the hell out of here."

Cord gestured curtly to the ranch hands he had brought with him from Antlers, and the three of them filed out, glaring at Chadwick and Matt. A moment later the sound of hoofbeats could be heard as they rode off.

Matt hurried over to Juan, who was still sitting on the floor with his back against the half-rotted wall of the shack. Kneeling beside him, Matt asked, "Are you all right, Juan?"

"*Sí*. Those *gringos*, they came in and . . . and scared me. They knocked me down, and the one called Cord shot a bullet into the ground at my feet. I thought they were going to hurt me."

"We won't let anybody hurt you, Juan," Chadwick

The Diablo Grant

promised as he slid his Colt back into its holster. "Tell you what—you'd better move out of this place and come on down to my house. I've got a spare room where you can stay until all this is over."

Matt thought that was an excellent suggestion. He said, "Yes, Juan, why don't you do that?"

The old man blinked at him. "I . . . I find myself doing things these days that I never thought I would do. But this is my home. I want to stay."

"Cord Richmond and his men may come back," Chadwick warned. "Ben Tompkins might send somebody after you, too. You'll be a lot safer staying with me."

Finally Juan nodded. "I will do this. But someone must tell Dolores where I am. She will worry if she comes here and cannot find me."

"I'll tell her," Matt promised. "As soon as I see her, I'll tell her you've gone to stay with Mr. Chadwick."

A new voice said from the doorway, "Here, now, what's all this?"

Matt and Chadwick looked around and saw a thick-bodied man in an expensive suit standing there. His face was full and florid, the hair under his brown hat was full, crisp, and white, and he had an air of respectability and affluence about him that was reinforced by the silver-headed walking stick he had clenched in one pudgy fist.

"Hello, Mr. Wells," Matt greeted him. "What are you doing here?"

"I was just leaving the bank when I saw Cord Richmond and a couple of his father's hands go riding past. They seemed angry, and they looked like they were in a hurry. Someone told me there was a shooting here and that the two of you had come running in this direction." Edmund Wells, owner of the local bank and mayor of Garrison, glared at them. "As the duly elected leader of the community, I have a right to know what's going on. This is something else to do with that blasted land grant, isn't it?"

Billy Chadwick grunted. "You must've seen the paper."

"Indeed I did." Wells took a folded copy from a coat pocket. He looked sternly at Matt and went on, "This is an incredible story, young man. I suppose you have proof of all the amazing claims Señor Espina here is making."

"We think we have sufficient proof," Chadwick said before Matt could reply. "And since I'm representing Señor Espina, I think it would be best if I took him down to my house and let him get some rest. I'm sure he's tired."

"Hmmph. Yes, I suppose so," Wells said. "And I suppose that Cord Richmond and his cronies came here to persuade the old man not to follow through with this case?"

"Something like that." Chadwick snorted. "If they had gotten their hands on the actual land grant documents, I reckon that would've been all right with them, too. I've had my assistant write out copies of the grant, but they wouldn't carry any legal weight. Only the original would do that."

"And where is it?" asked Wells.

"A safe place," Chadwick replied.

Wells grunted and nodded his leonine head. "Probably best that you keep that information to yourself, Mr. Chadwick." He switched his gaze to Matt. "I hope you're happy with yourself, young man. You've managed to stir up this whole part of the country. I fear that tonight is only the beginning of the trouble."

Matt shrugged. "I was just trying to help Juan, and as for putting the story in the paper, well, the people have a right to know, don't they? There's such a thing as freedom of the press."

"And sometimes it's more trouble than it's worth," Wells complained. "When do you expect this case to be settled, Counselor?"

"As soon as we can get a judge in here to hear the evidence," Chadwick replied. "I've wired the territorial capital, and the governor told me he'd get in touch with the attorney general in Washington. Since this is all tied up with the Treaty of Guadalupe Hidalgo, neither the local nor the territorial courts have jurisdiction. A federal circuit court judge will have to hear the case."

"Then I hope for the sake of the town that he gets here soon." Wells shook his head. "Because I can tell you this, gentlemen—I fear this situation is going to get much worse before it gets any better."

Juan gave a little whine of dismay, and Matt thought gloomily that the mayor, stuffy as he was, might be right.

Chapter Three

The big man on the Appaloosa stallion reined up in front of Garrison's biggest and best hotel six days later. He swung down from the saddle, looped the reins of the distinctively marked horse over the hitch rail, tossed his saddlebags over his shoulder, and stepped up onto the hotel porch. Appaloosas were uncommon in this part of the country, and the horse drew curious stares from the people on the street.

So did the man who had been riding him.

The stranger was of medium height, but his burly build and broad shoulders made him seem a little shorter. His light gray Stetson was pushed back slightly on hair that was thinning and turning gray. He had a well-trimmed, salt-and-pepper beard and mustache, and brown eyes that didn't miss much—if anything—as he looked up and down the street. He wore a long

The Diablo Grant

duster over a black vest, a faded red bib-front shirt, denim pants, and boots that had seen plenty of wear, like his saddle. Two long holsters were attached to that saddle, one containing a Winchester, the other a short-barreled, heavy-gauge shotgun. Riding in the holster on the cartridge belt strapped around the man's ample waist was a LeMat, the so-called grapeshot revolver, which featured a second barrel under the regular one so that in addition to standard .41-caliber cartridges the gun could also fire a single .62-caliber shotgun round. Some folks might have said the stranger was loaded for bear hunting, especially in this day and age. The Lincoln County War had ended several years earlier, the Santa Fe Ring had been broken up, and by and large the New Mexico Territory had settled down a mite.

Swatting trail dust off his clothes, Earl Stark went into the lobby of the hotel. The bespectacled clerk behind the desk, whose hair was pomaded and parted in the middle, frowned disapprovingly as Stark approached. The big, bearded man had the look of an aimless drifter, maybe even a hardcase on the dodge from the law. He couldn't have come to Garrison for any reason other than to cause trouble, the clerk decided.

Nervously the clerk asked, "Is there something I can do for you, sir?"

It was obvious to Stark that the man hoped the answer was no. Well, he would have to be disappointed. "Need a room," Stark said as he deposited his saddlebags on the counter, drawing another frown of dismay from the clerk. "And some information, too."

"I don't believe we have a room available right now—" the clerk began.

Stark laid a big hand on the hotel register and spun it around. Only a couple of names had been signed in the past week, and one of them he recognized: Alfred Fanning. He looked at the key rack and saw over a dozen keys hanging there.

"Reckon everybody must be out for the day," he said, "judging from the number of keys up there. Either that or you're lying to me." His voice was mild, but there was a steely edge to it.

"Well, perhaps I can find something . . ."

"Thought you could," Stark said genially. "Now, about the information."

The clerk sighed. "What do you want to know?"

"Where can I find Billy Chadwick?"

The clerk's eyebrows arched in surprise. "Mr. Chadwick's office is two blocks down and on the other side of the street, above the general store. You shouldn't have any trouble finding it."

"Thanks," grunted Stark. "What room're you putting me in?"

"Uh, how about seventeen? That's up on the first floor, in front."

Stark nodded and shoved the saddlebags across the counter. "That'll do fine. Have somebody take these up there and leave 'em for me."

"But I can't be responsible for—"

"What's your name?" Stark cut in.

"William, sir."

Stark grinned. "Well, William, I'm not worried. I don't reckon you'll let anything happen to my bags, will you?"

There was nothing the clerk could do but nod, then

The Diablo Grant

shake his head. "Yes, sir—I mean, no, sir. Of course not."

"Good." Stark started to turn away.

The clerk said, "Excuse me, sir, you'll have to sign the register."

"Almost forgot." Stark picked up the pen lying next to the open book, dipped its point in the inkwell, and scrawled *Earl Stark* under the other names. In the space for home address he wrote *Buffalo Flat, Texas,* even though he hadn't actually lived in Buffalo Flat for a long time. But he supposed it was the closest thing to home for a man who was on the trail nearly all the time. He laid the pen down and reached inside the duster. "One more thing. You ever seen this gent before?"

He took out a small, worn photograph and held it so that the clerk could see it. The picture showed a man sitting in a chair, dressed in a duster and range clothes and holding a rifle. The man was young and innocent-looking. The clerk studied the photograph for a moment, then shook his head. "I'm sorry. I don't know him."

"Didn't really figure you would," the big man said as he tucked the picture away again.

With a wave to the still-nervous clerk, Stark left the hotel lobby and started down the street toward the office of Billy Chadwick. He would have to put the Appaloosa in the hotel's livery, if it had one, or find a public stable if it didn't. But that could wait until after he had talked to Chadwick and found out just what he was dealing with here in Garrison.

Chadwick's office was where the hotel clerk had told

him it would be, in the same sort of upstairs room in which many prairie dog lawyers conducted their business. Stark went up the outside stairs, rapped sharply on the closed door at the landing, and went in without waiting for a reply when he found the door was unlocked. A man in shirtsleeves, vest, and string tie was sitting behind a desk with several books open in front of him. He looked up with a scowl of annoyance at Stark and snapped, "What is it?"

"You Billy Chadwick?" Stark asked.

"That's right."

"I'm Judge Earl Stark."

Chadwick stared at him for several seconds, taking in the dusty trail clothes and the gun belt strapped around his waist. Finally he said, "Judge?"

"That's right. Federal circuit judge for the Southwestern District." Stark took out a wallet and extracted some papers from it. "Here're my bona fides, if you've got any doubts."

Chadwick took the documents and examined them intently, then handed them back a moment later. "I've heard of you, of course, Your Honor. But I wasn't expecting—"

"Expecting me to look like some sort of range bum, Counselor?" Stark grinned. "That's all right. I like to be comfortable while I'm on the trail, and my job keeps me on horseback a lot. I've been threatening to get a buggy to ride around in, but I just haven't gotten to it yet. Anyway, I reckon that'd make me feel a mite older than I want to."

Chadwick stood up and extended a hand across the desk. "Well, I'm glad to meet you, Judge. Have a seat."

Stark shook hands with the lawyer, then settled him-

The Diablo Grant

self in a red leather chair in front of the desk. He tossed his Stetson onto a hat rack beside the door with an expert flip of the wrist. "Tell me what brings me here to Garrison," he said.

Chadwick hesitated as he sat down. "That's sort of irregular, isn't it? The evidence in a case is usually presented in an actual hearing. Not that I need to tell you that, Your Honor."

"Yep, I've read *Practice and Pleading* a few times myself. But nobody's ever accused me of being anything but an irregular judge, so you go ahead, Counselor. Not the details, just the lay of the land. I'll stop you if you start getting into areas you don't need to yet."

"All right." Chadwick nodded. "The case revolves around an old Spanish land grant . . ."

For the next few minutes Chadwick sketched out the basic facts of the case involving Juan Espina and the ownership of the Diablo Valley. Stark listened attentively, nodding occasionally.

When Chadwick was finished, Stark said, "All right, I reckon I've got a handle on it. The wire from the attorney general simply instructed me to come here and settle a property dispute, but I figured there was a little more to it than that. Sounds like an interesting case." He put his hands on his knees and shoved himself to his feet. "I'll hold a hearing as soon as possible. How's tomorrow morning sound?"

Chadwick looked a little surprised, but he nodded. "That'll be fine with us. I'm not sure how the other side will feel about it."

"I saw where Alfred Fanning checked in at the hotel," Stark said. "I've never had him argue a case in front of my bench before, but I've heard that he's pretty good. Rumor had it he was tied in with the Santa Fe Ring, but nobody was ever able to prove anything."

"And I wouldn't impugn the reputation of opposing counsel by intimating such a thing," Chadwick said.

Stark chuckled. "You don't have to, because I already did. But I'll check with Fanning anyway and make sure he's ready to go tomorrow morning. There a courthouse here in town?"

Chadwick shook his head. "No, but there's a town hall we can use. It should accommodate a good-sized crowd."

"Expecting quite a few spectators, are you?"

"I wouldn't be surprised. This case has been going on for about a week now, and that's enough time for folks to choose sides. There are plenty of people, smaller settlers mostly, who wouldn't mind seeing Juan Espina win."

"Well, we'll see how it comes out." Stark took out the photograph of the young man again. "Before I go, would you mind looking at this? Ever run across this fella before?"

Chadwick took the picture, studied it, then shook his head and handed it back. "Can't say as I have. Who is he?"

"That's what I'm trying to find out. He was . . . killed a while back in a dust-up I was involved in, and I promised myself I'd try to find out his name and where his family is, so I could tell them what happened to him."

"Well, good luck, but that's going to be kind of hard with nothing to go on but a photograph."

Stark shook his head ruefully. "That's what I've found out. But I'll keep trying, anyway." He put the

The Diablo Grant

picture away. "See you in the morning at the town hall. Nine o'clock, unless you hear different from me."

"My client and I will be there." Chadwick added, "You ought to talk to Matt Curry if you get a chance. He's the editor of the local newspaper and the one who found the land grant in the first place. He might know something about that youngster in the picture you're carrying."

"I'll do that," Stark said. "Thanks."

He plucked his hat from the rack and went out. He felt an instinctive liking for Billy Chadwick, sensing that the lawyer was a frontiersman like himself. Now he had to go see Chadwick's opponent, Alfred Fanning, who was reputed to be the kind of slick, smooth-talking, slippery-fingered gent who would have become a dishonest riverboat gambler if he hadn't taken up the law instead. Sometimes, despite his own experience as an attorney, Stark thought there wasn't much difference between the two professions.

But he wasn't going to let a personal bias color his judgment. He had never done that before, and he didn't intend to start in Garrison. Earl Stark was here to uphold law and order, by God, and that was just what he was going to do. It might not be easy, but then again, it hardly ever was.

Since he already knew Fanning by reputation, Stark decided to take care of some chores first. He turned the Appaloosa over to the stove-up old bronco buster who ran the stable behind the hotel, who promised to take good care of the horse. Stark believed him; the hostler had a gleam in his eye when he looked at the magnificent Appaloosa, and Stark recognized him as a gent who loved good horses. Then he returned to the hotel, pulled a change of clothes from his saddlebags, and went down the street to the barbershop to get his beard trimmed and take a bath in one of the big metal tubs in the shop's back room. Chances were, Fanning would take him seriously if he more closely resembled what a judge was supposed to look like. Putting on a suit and tie was a puredee pain in the rump, but sometimes it was worth it, Stark supposed.

A little later, he looked about as distinguished as he was ever going to when he knocked on the door of Alfred Fanning's room. A deep, resonant voice answered. "Who's there?"

"Judge Earl Stark."

The door swung open. The man who stood there was composed, but Stark could see the surprise in his eyes. He was perhaps fifty years old and still handsome, with thick, silvery hair and a narrow mustache. His coat was off at the moment, but his vest, shirt, and trousers were both impeccable and expensive, and his cravat was of the finest silk, held in place by a diamond stickpin. He smelled of bay rum and powder, and Stark had the feeling he was the sort of fellow who had himself shaved two or three times a day when he had the chance. There was no doubt in Stark's mind that he was looking at Alfred Fanning.

The man confirmed that by smiling and saying, "Please, come in, Your Honor. I've been looking forward to meeting you. I'm Alfred Fanning."

"Figured as much," Stark grunted. He took the hand Fanning offered and found it cool and smooth. The grip was firm enough, if fleeting. Stark went on, "I came to tell you that the hearing on Juan Espina's case will be at nine o'clock tomorrow morning, if that's all right with you."

Fanning frowned slightly as he motioned Stark toward an armchair. Stark sat down and looked around the room, which was furnished as opulently as a good-sized cattle-town hotel could manage. He was sure there were much fancier places in Santa Fe, but Fanning seemed comfortable as he settled himself in another armchair and steepled his fingers in front of his face.

"To be honest with you, Your Honor, I wasn't expecting the hearing to begin quite so soon."

"No point in wasting time," Stark said briskly. "That is, unless you're not ready to present your client's case, Counselor."

"Oh, I'm ready," Fanning replied casually. "And I'm sure you'll agree that it has merit. Actually, I have two clients, Your Honor. I represent Mr. Travis Richmond and Mr. Benjamin Tompkins. Two very fine gentlemen, if I may be allowed to say so. The salt of the earth. I don't believe it's too much to say that they've made Diablo Valley the virtual paradise that it is today, Judge Stark. They brought progress and civilization to a land that was little more than a wilderness when they arrived. With their own hands, with their own blood and sweat, each of my clients has created a veritable empire. I'm sure you'll agree, Your Honor, that this territory—this very nation—was carved out by men of just such hardiness and vision."

"Not a bad opening statement, Mr. Fanning," Stark said dryly, "but I'd appreciate it if you'd save the rest of it for tomorrow."

Fanning smiled and inclined his head in acknowledgment of Stark's point. "I'm afraid I do get carried away sometimes in my quest for justice," he said. "Especially when the case is so open and shut and involves such fine men as my clients."

Stark stood up. "Well, we'll see. Nine o'clock at the town hall."

"We'll be there, Your Honor. I look forward to it."

"Yeah," Stark grunted. He was looking forward to it, too, even more so now that he knew Fanning was exactly the kind of fast-talking hombre he had expected him to be. The lawyer from Santa Fe was as unlike Billy Chadwick as he could be. This case was likely going to have some ramifications that Stark wouldn't be too happy with, but he was going to enjoy watching Chadwick and Fanning go at each other in court.

After leaving Fanning's room, Stark decided he had time to pay a visit to the newspaper editor Chadwick had mentioned. The desk clerk downstairs, who seemed a mite friendlier now that Stark had cleaned up and put on a suit, told him where to find the office of the *Territorial Observer*.

The place smelled of printer's ink. A young man was working at a desk behind a wooden railing that divided the front room in half. He looked up as Stark entered and asked, "Can I help you?"

Stark said, "You'd be Matt Curry, I expect." He came through a gate in the railing and held out his hand over the desk. "I'm Judge Earl Stark, here to hold a hearing on this land grant case."

Curry popped up out of his chair and enthusiastically shook Stark's hand. "I'm glad to meet you, Your Honor. It's not often we get a federal judge holding

The Diablo Grant

court here in Garrison. Never until now, in fact." He grinned. He was a good-looking young man with dark hair and an alert, intelligent face. Not long on experience, Stark decided, but open-minded and anxious to learn.

"I hear you're the one who found the old land grant documents and figured out what they were."

"That's right," Curry said with a nod.

"And you've been playing up the story in your newspaper, too. I was shown a copy of it in Santa Fe when I was passing through on my way here."

Curry shrugged. "It's certainly important enough to warrant a story in the paper, don't you think, Judge Stark?"

"Oh, I'm not arguing that," Stark said. "If the land grant holds up, it's going to affect everybody who lives in Diablo Valley, not to mention you folks down here in Garrison."

"I know," Curry said. "I expect it'll have a lot of repercussions."

"And that doesn't bother you?"

Curry frowned. "Why should it?"

"You got the ball to rolling when you found that land grant," Stark pointed out.

"All I did was recognize it for what it was. That, and take old Juan to see Billy Chadwick so he could find out what his legal rights are. He was entitled to that, don't you think?"

Stark wasn't going to argue the point, although he figured Matt Curry had been more interested in the news value of the story he'd accidentally uncovered than in Juan Espina's legal rights. He said, "We'll be hashing out those legal rights tomorrow morning. The hearing's set for nine o'clock at the town hall. You'll have to be there."

"Of course," Curry said. "I'll be covering the hearing for the newspaper."

"You'll be a witness, too," Stark told him. "After all, you're the one who found those documents. All that has to be established in testimony."

"I'll be there," Curry promised.

That about wrapped up Stark's official business with the young editor, but before he left he hauled out the photograph again and showed it to Curry. "When I knew this young fella," he explained, "he was just called the Kid. I'm trying to find out who he really was. I need to find his kinfolk, if he had any, and let them know what happened to him. He went bad . . . died at the end of a rope."

"Wish I could help you, Your Honor. But I'm afraid I've never seen this man before."

Stark nodded, a little disappointed but not surprised. He had been searching for some clue to the Kid's real identity for a long time without success. It would be easy to give in to that disappointment and figure that he would never find out who the Kid really was. That wasn't Stark's way, though. He would keep looking, keep asking questions, and one of these days he would have the answers that had so far eluded him. He was sure of it.

In the meantime he had a hearing to conduct, and he would need a clear head for that. Which meant he would need a good night's sleep, and in order to get that, he had to have a good supper. That need prompted him to ask Matt Curry where to find the best eatery in

The Diablo Grant

town, and the editor's directions sent him to a restaurant owned by a big Swede with a huge sweep of blond mustaches who chicken-fried steaks that seemed damn near as big as a whole side of beef, which he served with mountains of fried potatoes, plenty of gravy and biscuits, and generous dollops of sweet butter and honey.

Stark ate well, slept well, and rose the next morning ready to dispense justice to the best of his ability.

As usual, it didn't quite work out that way.

Chapter Four

Billy Chadwick had warned Stark that there would be a lot of people interested in the land grant hearing, but even so Stark was not prepared for the crowd he found at the town hall that morning. Folks were spilling out of the hall and crowding the porch that ran along the front of the building. Every foot of hitchrack space along the main street seemed to be occupied. All manner of vehicles, from fancy carriages with brass door handles to broken-down spring wagons, were tied side by side; big, fine horses with expensive saddles stood next to mules draped with woven blankets. Obviously this hearing had attracted all sorts.

That became even clearer as Stark approached the town hall. He saw store clerks in vests and sleeve garters, gamblers in lightweight suits and broad-brimmed

The Diablo Grant

hats, gun-hung cowboys wearing batwing chaps and high-crowned Stetsons, freighters in work boots and patched corduroy trousers, Mexican farmers in homespun cotton pants and tunics, a single black-suited minister, the local telegraph operator with his green eyeshade, a goodly number of sunbonneted women in calico dresses, and almost as many saloon girls in tight silk gowns and feathered hats. Children ran here and there, shouting and laughing, either not knowing or not caring what these proceedings would mean to the grown-ups around them. Where there were kids there were usually dogs, and today was no exception. The whole gathering reminded Stark of carnivals he had been to. Practically the entire town of Garrison had turned out to be enlightened, entertained, or both.

Chances were, they wouldn't be disappointed.

Stark made his way through the crowd. Most of the people there didn't know him, but they cleared a path for him anyway, deferring instinctively to his size and determination. He frowned at the cowboys clustered around the entrance. They were probably hands on the ranches owned by Richmond and Tompkins, the two cattlemen leading the opposition to Juan Espina's claim. Stark didn't want a dozen or more proddy, gun-toting rannies in any courtroom of his, even a temporary one like this. The cowboys would check their guns at the door with the local law, or they wouldn't come in.

When he reached the door and stepped inside, however, he saw that several punchers from the Box BT and Antlers spreads were already in the hall, and all of them were packing iron, of course. He grimaced. This was likely to be a problem, but since they were already inside he figured disarming them would be next to impossible.

At the front of the room a table had been set up that he could use for his bench, and facing it, side by side, were two smaller tables. Billy Chadwick was already sitting at one of them, and beside him was an old man in a black suit that had obviously been purchased recently. The old-timer looked uncomfortable as he put a finger inside the stiff collar of his white shirt and ran it around his skinny neck. He twisted his head from side to side, casting nervous glances over his shoulders at the crowd filling the room behind him.

At the other table was Alfred Fanning, along with two men in suits that were nowhere nearly as fancy or new as the one belonging to their lawyer. Stark took them to be Travis Richmond and Ben Tompkins and wondered which was which.

Stark pushed his way along the crowded aisle between the benches. There was a Bible on the table, he saw, along with a gavel. The local court probably met here. He had his own Bible, a small volume tucked inside his coat, but he would use the one on the table to swear in witnesses. He was about to decide he would have to act as his own bailiff, but then he spotted a man wearing a sheriff's badge, caught the man's eye, and gestured for him to come over.

"Judge Earl Stark," he said to the sheriff, raising his voice a little so that he could be heard over the din of voices filling the big room.

The lawman stuck out his hand. "I'm Sheriff Boone Higgins, Judge. Mighty pleased to meet you." He was about Stark's age, with a dark handlebar mustache and the beginnings of a beer gut. He looked as if he could

The Diablo Grant

still handle most problems that came his way, though.

Stark shook hands and said, "Reckon you could get me a little order in here?"

"Sure thing, Your Honor." Sheriff Higgins stepped up to the judge's table, picked up the gavel, and smacked it down on the hardwood surface several times. "Shut the hell up!" he bellowed at the top of his lungs. "Let's have some order in here, damn it!"

What the sheriff lacked in decorum he made up for in effectiveness, Stark thought as he looked down and wiped a hand across his mouth to hide his grin. At least Higgins hadn't hauled out the hogleg on his hip and blasted a couple of shots into the ceiling. Gradually the uproar in the hall died down, and Stark strode up to the table to take his place behind it. "Thanks, Sheriff," he said to Higgins as he took the gavel from him.

"Ever'body on your feet!" Higgins yelled. "This here is a special session of the federal circuit court of the United States of America, Judge Earl Stark presidin'. Now siddown an' keep your grub holes shut less'n the judge says otherwise."

Stark had to grin again as he sat down, and laughter rippled through the room. Evidently folks here in Garrison were aware that Sheriff Boone Higgins was something of an eccentric. Stark rapped the gavel a couple of times and said loudly, "This hearing will come to order." After another tap of the gavel he went on, "The purpose of it is to establish the legality of an alleged land grant giving possession of the area known as Diablo Valley to the heirs of one Emiliano Espina." He looked at the table where Billy Chadwick and the old man were sitting. "I take it this is your client, Mr. Chadwick?"

The lawyer rose to his feet. "That's correct, Your Honor. This is Señor Juan Espina."

Stark nodded and turned his attention to Alfred Fanning. "This is neither a criminal trial nor a civil lawsuit, Counselor. What's your status here?" Stark knew the answer, of course, but official procedure had to be followed.

Fanning stood up, nodded urbanely, and said, "Amicus curiae, Your Honor. I'm here as a friend of the court, representing the two gentlemen who have an interest in the case at hand. This is Mr. Travis Richmond"—Fanning indicated the lean, gray-haired man beside him—"and Mr. Benjamin Tompkins." Tompkins was the barrel-chested gent, Stark noted. Fanning went on, "Mr. Richmond and Mr. Tompkins have retained my services on their behalf, as well as on the behalf of the other ranchers in the area known as Diablo Valley."

Stark knew from his talk with Billy Chadwick that the other spreads in Diablo Valley didn't amount to much. Richmond and Tompkins were the big skookum he-wolves around here, and they were accustomed to getting their way.

He nodded, leaned back in his chair, and said, "All right, Mr. Chadwick, you may proceed."

Before Chadwick could do so, however, a commotion at the back of the room made Stark look up and everyone else in the town hall turn around. A couple of men carrying rifles and wearing Mexican army uniforms strode into the room, forcing a path through the crowd and drawing curses and angry comments in the process. Sheriff Higgins, standing near the judge's table, exclaimed, "What the hell! Mexico must be invadin' us again!" and reached for his gun.

The Diablo Grant

"Wait a minute, Sheriff!" Stark ordered. He didn't want gunplay in a room packed with innocent people, and besides, it didn't seem likely Mexico would send an invasion force consisting of two *federales* across the border. Also, Stark had spotted two more people following the soldiers, and they didn't look like invaders, either.

One of the civilian newcomers was a middle-aged man with sleek, dark hair, noble features, and a thin mustache. His short jacket and trousers were elegantly cut and obviously expensive, as was the ruffled silk shirt under the jacket. In his left hand he carried a black, flat-brimmed hat. He looked like a wealthy *hacendado*, but Stark sensed there was more to him than that.

The young woman with him was stunning, with a mane of thick, midnight-black hair and a strong, slender figure that was displayed to advantage in a form-fitting, dark green traveling outfit. A lace mantilla in the Spanish style was draped over her shoulders. Her beauty caused almost as much of a stir as did the soldiers with their rifles.

Stark picked up the gavel and hammered on the table, trying to quiet down the crowd. Sheriff Higgins assisted by bellowing, "Hush up, consarn it!"

The *federales* marched up the aisle and then stepped to the sides so that they flanked the older man and the young woman as they approached the judge's table. Stark stared at them, flabbergasted.

"*Buenos dias,* Your Honor," the man said. "You are the judge in charge of this case, no?"

"I am the judge in this case, yes," Stark stated, laying his palms flat on the table. "Judge Earl Stark."

"Allow me to introduce myself. I am Don Alfonso Montoya, representing the government of His Excellency, *Presídente* Porfirio Díaz." The man bowed to Stark.

With a frown, Stark asked, "And the young lady?"

"My daughter Angelina," Montoya said with a somewhat irritated glance at the young woman. Stark had a feeling it wasn't Montoya's idea that his daughter accompany him here.

Alfred Fanning was on his feet. "Your Honor, I'd like to know the meaning of this interruption," he said testily.

"So would I," Stark agreed. "Are you here on business, Señor Montoya?"

"Indeed I am," the aristocratic Mexican replied. "I am here to represent the interests of the Republic of Mexico in the matter of the disputed Espina land grant."

Stark's frown deepened. "How did the Mexican government know—" He broke off the question with a shake of his head. "Never mind. I reckon your President Díaz has folks in Santa Fe keeping an ear to the ground for him."

Montoya smiled thinly and inclined his head a little. That was as close to an acknowledgement that the Mexican government had spies in Santa Fe as Stark was likely to get, and he knew it. Montoya must have burned up the roads from Mexico City to reach Garrison so quickly.

Stark went on, "This case falls under the jurisdiction of the United States federal court, Señor Montoya. I'm not sure exactly what interest President Díaz thinks the Mexican government has in the matter."

The Diablo Grant

"The case involves the possession of land granted to the Espina family by the king of Spain, as I am certain you are already aware, Your Honor. That royal grant is regarded as legal and binding by my government, and we hope you share that opinion. We are interested only in justice, Judge Stark."

Stark nodded slowly. The Mexican government was interested in setting a precedent, he thought. If his decision upheld the legality of the land grant, it would be that much easier for Mexico to obtain favorable decisions in other cases later that involved American versus Mexican interests. From everything Stark had heard about the Mexican dictator, Díaz was a crude, ruthless son of a bitch, but he was cunning, too. He had to be, to hang on to power in that hotbed of revolution below the border.

This was an added complication, but Stark saw no way of getting out of it. He said to Montoya, "All right, Señor Montoya, I'll allow you to take part in these proceedings as a friend of the court. Why don't you sit down at the table with Señor Espina and Mr. Chadwick?"

"Of course. Thank you, Your Honor."

Stark jerked a thumb at the two *federales*. "I reckon these boys are part of your escort?"

"That is correct."

"Send 'em back outside. No offense, Señor, but *I* maintain order in this courtroom."

"Certainly." Montoya turned to the soldiers and issued an order in crisp, rapid Spanish. The two men saluted and marched back down the aisle and out of the town hall. Stark wondered how many more troops Montoya had brought with him. He hoped not many;

folks would get nervous with a bunch of foreign soldiers hanging around. He didn't want this hearing to turn into an international squabble.

Following Stark's orders, Sheriff Higgins commandeered a couple of chairs from the spectators and placed them at the table with Billy Chadwick and Juan Espina. Don Alfonso and his daughter sat down, and Stark tried to remember where in the proceedings he had been when this latest interruption occurred. He was about to tell Chadwick to get on with presenting his case when Fanning popped up again and said, "Objection, Your Honor."

"To what?" Stark asked.

"You've allowed this Mexican gentleman the same status as an American citizen," Fanning said. Although his tone was smooth and civil, he was clearly outraged. "A Mexican national should not be accorded the standing of a friend of the court in an American judicial proceeding."

"Why not?" Stark shot back. "There's no law against it, as far as I know, so long as he's got a legitimate reason for being here."

Fanning raised an eyebrow. "Well . . . perhaps you're correct, Your Honor. I'll withdraw the objection."

Stark's jaw tightened, and his eyes narrowed in anger. Fanning had played that well. Knowing he had no legal grounds for the objection, he had still managed to call into question Stark's competence and knowledge of the law while appealing to the ill will that many white settlers bore for Mexicans generally. Stark could hear murmurs of agreement among the spectators as Fanning spoke. He grunted morosely. Public opinion

The Diablo Grant

had been known to sway more than one judge in a tricky case.

Fanning had bitten off more than he'd figured on by pulling such a fancy trick, however. Stark hoped he knew that. If he didn't, he would soon.

Stark looked at Billy Chadwick. "I think we're finally ready, Mr. Chadwick," he said.

"Thank you, Your Honor. Our case is simple and straightforward. I have only two witnesses and one piece of evidence to present, but I'm sure that will be enough."

"Speak your piece," Stark said, leaning back again and lacing his fingers together over his belly.

As Chadwick had promised, his presentation was brief. He called Matthew Curry to the stand—a chair at one end of Stark's table—and asked him to relate how the land grant had come to light. Curry testified that he had been helping Juan Espina back to the old man's shack one night when Juan wasn't feeling well. Stark knew that meant Juan had been drunk as a skunk, but that wasn't relevant. Curry told how he had found the documents in question in the Espina family Bible.

Stark sat forward. "Are these papers in your possession, Mr. Chadwick?"

"Yes, Your Honor, they are. I want to present them in evidence right now." Chadwick opened a leather case on the table in front of him and took out several sheets of parchment that were yellow and crackly with age. He came around the table and brought them up to Stark, who took them carefully. Chadwick asked, "Do you read Spanish, Your Honor?"

"Yes, I do. I'll want a copy of your translation of

these documents, though, Counselor, just to make sure we're in agreement on what they say."

Fanning spoke up. "I'd like to take a look at those papers, Your Honor."

"Then come on up here and look at 'em. I'm not handing them over to you, though, if that's what you're after."

Stark saw a flicker of irritation in Fanning's eyes. He knew good and well the lawyer wouldn't try anything as crude and obvious as "accidentally" destroying the land grant papers, but if Fanning could slip in a shot or two, so could Earl Stark. He went on, "I'm sure Mr. Chadwick's clerk wrote out several copies, in both English and Spanish, so you can have a couple of them."

"That's fine with us, Your Honor," Chadwick said. He went back to his table to fetch the copies.

Once that was sorted out and Fanning was studying the documents with his two clients, Stark glanced at the original parchment sheets himself, not searching for particulars but simply satisfying himself that they did indeed appear to be a land grant of some kind.

"Proceed, Mr. Chadwick," he said.

Under Chadwick's questioning, Matt Curry told how he had brought Juan to see the lawyer and start the process of claiming the land. As soon as Chadwick was done with his witness, Fanning was on his feet.

"I'd like to cross-examine, Your Honor."

"This is a hearing, not a trial," Stark pointed out. "But if you've got some questions, Mr. Fanning, go ahead and ask 'em."

"Thank you, Your Honor." Fanning clasped his hands behind his back and strolled out from behind the table where his clients sat. "Mr. Curry, you are the editor of the local newspaper, are you not?"

"I already said that's what I do for a living," Curry replied impatiently. His dislike for Fanning was obvious.

"And you have featured the story of this land grant and the resulting hearing quite prominently in your paper, haven't you?"

"Of course I have. It's news."

"What is your father's name, Mr. Curry?"

The young editor frowned and looked at Stark. "What's that got to do with all this?" he asked. "Do I have to answer?"

"Go ahead," Stark said. "I'd like to know the connection myself."

Curry hesitated a couple of seconds, then said, "My father is Edward Farrington Curry."

Fanning smiled. "The owner, publisher, and editor of several large newspapers back east? That is the Edward Farrington Curry of whom you speak?"

"Sure. That's no secret."

Fanning paced back and forth a few steps and said, "Then tell me, Mr. Curry, if you are in the newspaper business yourself, why aren't you back east working for your father?"

"I decided not to," Curry answered tightly. "I wanted to make a career in journalism for myself, not ride on my father's coattails."

"To make a name for yourself, to come out from under the shadow of your illustrious father, is that it, Mr. Curry?"

"I guess you could put it that way."

"And this so-called land grant story—that's going

to make a name for you, isn't it, Mr. Curry? That's what you intended all along, isn't it?"

"What are you saying?" Curry shot back, his voice rising with anger. "That I faked those documents just so I could come up with a big story for the *Observer*? That's ridiculous!"

Stark thought so, too, and when the spectators began talking excitedly, Stark gaveled them back to order before the disruption could spread. He said loudly, "These documents look genuine enough to me, Mr. Fanning. Unless you have some proof that Mr. Curry is responsible for their existence, you'd better try another trail."

"Certainly, Your Honor. Nothing further."

"Go sit down," Stark told Curry. "What's next, Mr. Chadwick?"

"I call Juan Espina to the stand, Your Honor," Chadwick said.

The old-timer was scared. Stark could see that plain as day. After Juan was sworn in, he sat down awkwardly, his right hand trembling on the Bible held by Sheriff Higgins. Stark leaned over and asked gently, "You speak English all right, Juan?"

"*Sí*, señor. I have lived here in New Mexico all my life."

"All right. Go ahead, Mr. Chadwick."

Swiftly Chadwick established that Juan Espina was the great-great-great-grandson of Emiliano Espina, who was named in the land grant from the king of Spain. The family Bible, with its section of records filled out in faded ink, confirmed that. Stark looked at the Bible, showed it to Fanning, who merely grunted in acknowledgment of the point, then gave it back to

The Diablo Grant

Chadwick. Next, in his halting voice, Juan explained that he was the only surviving member of his family.

Stark said, "Hold on a minute. When I was looking at that Bible, I thought it said you were married and had a daughter."

"My wife and my child. They both died many years ago, Señor Stark—*perdone,* I mean Your Honor."

"That's all right. Sorry about your loss, Juan."

"So," Chadwick said, "you are not only a legal descendant of Emiliano Espina, Juan, but you are the *sole* surviving descendant?"

"Sí."

Chadwick turned to Stark. "That's all we have, Your Honor. If you'll study the documents, you'll see that the case is cut and dried. Under the terms of the land grant, the area known then as Diablo Valley—and still known as Diablo Valley—is and rightfully should be the property of my client, Juan Espina."

Stark looked at Fanning, who stood up and said, "I have one question for this witness, Your Honor."

"Ask it."

"Señor Espina, are you sober today?"

Chadwick glared at the other lawyer. "Objection!"

"Sit down, Fanning," Stark said coldly. "The objection is sustained."

Fanning shrugged. It was a point he didn't really have to make, Stark supposed. Everybody in the room probably knew that Juan Espina was the town drunk. But that fact had no legal bearing on the case.

Stark turned his attention to Don Alfonso, who had been watching the proceedings intently. "Do you have anything you want to say, Señor Montoya?"

The Mexican representative stood up and bowed.

"Thank you, Your Honor. Indeed I do. I can tell you that another copy of the Espina land grant exists in the national archives in Mexico City. I did not bring it with me, but I have seen it with my own eyes, and I can testify that it grants ownership of Diablo Valley to Emiliano Espina and his heirs."

Stark grunted. "I'm not doubting your word, Don Alfonso, but it'd carry a little more weight if you had the other copy of the grant with you."

Montoya shrugged eloquently. "It was decided that for safekeeping it would be best to leave the document in the archives."

"Anything else?"

"No, Your Honor." Montoya sat down again.

Stark looked at Fanning and his clients. It was their turn now. "Go ahead, Mr. Fanning."

"Thank you, Your Honor. I call Travis Richmond to the stand."

As the tall, gray-haired cattleman stood up, Stark warned, "This had better have something to do with the case."

"It does, Your Honor," Fanning said. "It has everything to do with the case."

Stark nodded and leaned back again.

After the rancher had been sworn in, Fanning asked, "How long have you lived in the area known as Diablo Valley, Mr. Richmond?"

"Almost thirty years," Richmond replied. "I started Antlers—that's my spread—back in the fifties."

"And it's been your home ever since?"

"It has. My son Cord was born there. I've buried a wife and three other children there." Richmond's voice was steady, but Stark could see the strain on his face,

The Diablo Grant

even though the rancher looked straight ahead and showed only his profile to Stark. He went on, "Damn right it's my home."

"How did you acquire the land?"

"Claimed it from the government, homesteaded it, held it against Apaches and droughts and blizzards. Like every other rancher in these parts."

"And you did all of this—poured your heart and your soul, your sweat and your blood, into this land—all in good faith that it was indeed *yours*?"

"That's right."

Fanning's voice was soft as he asked, "Why did you do this, Mr. Richmond?"

"Because I wanted to leave something behind for my son and my grandson and all the others down the line." For the first time, Richmond looked at Stark. "I wanted to build something that nobody could ever take away from them."

Stark's expression was grim. He felt the accusation in Travis Richmond's eyes, saw the pain of betrayal there. Richmond was the kind of rock-solid settler who had made something out of nothing, who through sheer grit had brought civilization to the frontier. Stark had known dozens, maybe hundreds, just like him, and he respected every one of them to some extent. In his younger days Stark had cowboyed for men like Richmond, had ridden night herd with them, had saved their lives and been saved by them in turn. Travis Richmond was a hell of a lot closer to Stark's roots, to who and what he was, than any set of laws.

But it was the law that Earl Stark was sworn to uphold.

"Go ahead if you've got anything else," he said grimly to Fanning.

The lawyer from Santa Fe wore a smirk. "I think that's all from Mr. Richmond."

Chadwick shook his head, indicating that he had no questions. The mood in the room had definitely swung against Juan Espina—not that there had been much sympathy for him in the first place other than from a few Mexican farmers who were crowded into a corner of the hall. Stark figured they were rooting for Juan; small farmers like that were always in danger of being crowded out by the big Anglo ranchers, and they doubtless hoped to see one of their own stand up to the cattlemen and win for a change.

"Go ahead," he said to Fanning.

"Just a few more questions, Your Honor, this time for my other client, Mr. Benjamin Tompkins."

Although he was not as well-spoken, Tompkins repeated essentially the same story as Richmond: decades of hard, dangerous work to establish his ranch, the Box BT. He had no family buried on his spread, no son to leave the place to, but his claim was just as strong as Richmond's. He had never doubted that the land he'd homesteaded was his and would remain his.

After Tompkins stepped down from the stand, Fanning launched into a speech. Stark had been expecting as much, and now he got it.

"Your Honor, I do not doubt even for an instant that you want to make the proper decision in this case. The law must be served. But so must justice, and I have to ask Your Honor how it would be even the most remote semblance of justice to rip the land known as Diablo Valley away from the men who have settled it, who have by the force of their own will and courage, by their sacrifice, turned it into perhaps the best ranching

The Diablo Grant

land in the entire territory, and hand it over—hand it over on a platter just like the head of John the Baptist was handed to Salome!—to a man who has done nothing, absolutely *nothing*, to earn it or claim possession of it. To a *Mexican* who can be found any night of the week crawling from cantina to cantina, drunk on tequila, a pitiful, broken excuse of a man who has no right to steal the fruits of other men's labor! I tell you, Your Honor, this would *not* be justice! This would be a terrible *in*justice! And I appeal to you, Your Honor, not to take away the life's work of not only these two good men but of all the other settlers of Diablo Valley who homesteaded their land in good faith. Remember, Your Honor, that simple but oh-so-important word: justice." Fanning took a deep, dramatic breath, then said, "Thank you," and sat down.

Applause thundered through the room. Men stamped their feet on the floor, whistled, and waved their hats in the air. It sounded like an old-fashioned political rally. Fanning could sway a crowd, Stark had to hand him that. And despite his dislike of the attorney from Santa Fe, Stark had to admit that he had made some good points. It *would* be unfair for Richmond and Tompkins and the other ranchers to lose their spreads just because of an old piece of paper that none of them knew existed until recently.

Unfair—but if those documents said what Stark thought they did, entirely legal.

He let the uproar run its course this time, not picking up the gavel until the noise was already starting to subside. He rapped it a couple of times on the table and, when the room was quiet again, asked Chadwick, "Anything else you want to say, Counselor?"

Chadwick rose slowly. "Only that I'm confident you'll follow the law in this case, Your Honor."

Stark nodded grimly. He gathered up the land grant papers, then said, "I'm going to study these documents. This hearing will reconvene tomorrow morning at nine o'clock, at which time I will render my decision." He cracked the gavel down against the table. "Hearing's adjourned!"

That provoked another commotion. Fanning shouted over the noise in the town hall, "Your Honor, surely you can't expect my clients to wait twenty-four hours for your decision!"

"By God, I'm not going to rush this!" Stark roared. "I said the hearing's adjourned, and damn it, it's *adjourned*! Sheriff Higgins, clear the room!"

"Yes, sir, Your Honor!" the lawman said, and this time he brought his revolver out of its holster. The gun blasted three times into the ceiling, shocking the room into silence. "The judge said clear out!" Higgins bellowed.

Things were going to be mighty tense around here for the rest of the day and the night to come, Stark thought as he surveyed the crowd. People were going to be waiting anxiously for nine o'clock in the morning to roll around again.

And when it did, he mused, all hell just might break loose.

Chapter Five

Sheriff Higgins took Stark out the back door of the town hall to avoid the huge crowd still milling about in front. They kept to the alleys until they reached Stark's hotel.

"If you need anything, Your Honor, just let me know," Higgins told him. "I sure don't envy the job you've got to do now."

"I'm not looking forward to it myself," Stark admitted. "Thanks for your help, Sheriff."

He went in the rear entrance of the hotel and made it up to his room without anyone spotting him. Once there, he took off his coat and tie, kicked his boots aside, and sat down on the bed to study the land grant documents. He had a fair knowledge of Spanish, both written and spoken. The writing on the old parchment was the real thing, not the bastardized border lingo he was used to, but he was still able to wade through it without much trouble.

For the next couple of hours he pored over the documents. Once he got past all the fancy, archaic phrasing, he concluded that the papers said essentially what Matt Curry and Billy Chadwick claimed they did: The king of Spain had indeed granted Diablo Valley to Emiliano Espina and his heirs. Stark searched diligently for anything that rang false, any indication that the documents might have been faked. Although he wasn't an expert on these things, he had seen a lot of old, official papers, and he was convinced these were the genuine article.

Once that was cinched in his mind, he went to his saddlebags and brought out the copy of the Treaty of Guadalupe Hidalgo he had brought with him from Santa Fe, as well as copies of other court decisions that had arisen from disputes over the treaty's provisions. A few loopholes had rendered some of the old land grants invalid.

But by the time a couple more hours had passed, Stark had not only forgotten to eat lunch, he was also convinced that this was not one of those cases.

By law, Diablo Valley belonged to Juan Espina.

And that was exactly what Stark had been afraid of. He didn't want to take Antlers away from Travis Richmond or the Box BT away from Ben Tompkins. Those men, and the other ranchers in the valley, deserved better. And there was the question, too, of what in blazes Juan Espina would do with Diablo Valley if he had it. The old man was no rancher; the only thing he was capable of was getting drunk. Even Stark could see that.

The Diablo Grant

But the law was the law, and it had to be followed, Stark told himself. There had been a time—a moment of passion—when he hadn't followed the law, and that moment had haunted him for years now. With a sigh, he reached into his saddlebags and took out the small photograph.

"Kid, you were one sorry son of a bitch," he said to the deceptively innocent image in the picture, "but I reckon you've had your revenge on me. Every time I run across a case like this, I remember what happened back there in Ryanville. And I've got to do what the law says."

Even when he didn't want to.

Stark slipped down to the lobby and asked the clerk to have some food sent up to his room. A little later, when a knock sounded on the door, Stark expected it to be someone from the kitchen with a tray.

Instead, Matt Curry stood there, hat in hand, a hopeful expression on his face. "Hello, Judge Stark," he said quickly. "Can I talk to you for a few minutes?"

Stark frowned and looked up and down the hall. "Anybody with you?"

"No. The folks who work here at the hotel are doing their best to keep people from bothering you. But they don't know I'm up here. I slipped up the back way."

"Same as I did," Stark grunted. He opened the door wider. "Come on in, son. I reckon I've got a few minutes. But my lunch is supposed to be on the way, and I got to warn you, I'm hungry enough to eat a grizzly."

Curry grinned. "This shouldn't take long, Judge. I just want to ask you a couple of questions."

"Not about the case, I hope," Stark said sharply as

he closed the door. "I'm not going to talk about that."

"No, sir. I want to find out more about *you*."

Stark frowned. "Me? What is there to find out about me?"

"Well . . ." Curry slipped a pad of paper and a pencil from inside his coat. "I'm told that you were famous even before you became a judge. Is it true you used to be called Big Earl?"

"Wait just a dad-blasted minute," snapped Stark. "You planning on writing all this down and putting it in the paper?"

"With your permission, of course."

Stark folded his arms across his chest. "Well, you ain't got it. I'm here to render a decision in a difficult case, not to be played up in the newspaper like some sort of dime-novel hero."

"Are you sure?" Curry asked. "Some publicity might help your career."

Stark shook his head emphatically. "I'm doing what I want to do right now. Got no political ambitions, if that's what you're suggesting, son. I just want to be the best judge I can, and I don't need folks running around spouting tall tales about Big Earl."

With a sigh of regret, Curry put the paper and pencil away. "All right, Judge, if that's the way you want it. But will you answer a few questions anyway, just to satisfy my curiosity?"

"Depends on whether you'll answer some for me."

Curry nodded. "All right."

"Who told you I used to be called Big Earl?"

"Billy Chadwick mentioned it to me. He knew he had seen you somewhere before, and he finally remembered that you were the shotgun guard on a stagecoach

The Diablo Grant

he was riding once with a friend of his. They were carrying some money up to the Red River country in Texas, and some outlaws tried to stop the stage and hold it up." There was a touch of awe in the young editor's voice as he went on, "Mr. Chadwick said you blew two of them out of their saddles with your shotgun and killed the other man with that fancy pistol you carry. That's what finally made him remember you, that LeMat."

"I was doing my job, that's all," Stark said. "I'm afraid I don't remember Chadwick or his pard. But I was on a lot of runs where somebody got the dumb idea of trying to pull a holdup. That's what the stage lines paid me to stop."

"Mr. Chadwick said you were the best guard any of the stage lines ever had. And he wished you had been on the coach all the way to the Red River, because it did get held up later on, and the money he and his friend were delivering was stolen. They got it back, though."

Stark nodded. He hadn't known Billy Chadwick for long, but he wasn't surprised the leather-tough attorney wouldn't stand for having desperadoes make off with money he was responsible for.

Curry went on, "No offense, Judge, but I'd like to know how you went from stagecoach guard to federal judge."

"I wanted to make something more of myself," Stark answered honestly. "Found a set of law books on one of the coaches and studied them on my own. I became a lawyer that way. Later on I got appointed to the federal circuit court." He shrugged his broad shoulders. "That's about all there is to tell."

That wasn't quite true. He had wound up on the federal bench through the efforts of a congressman in Washington who puredee hated his guts; judges in the Southwestern District had a habit of not living very long. In the past they had been gunned down on a fairly regular basis by disgruntled lawyers, defendants, and plaintiffs. So far, Stark had frustrated his old enemy's plan for vengeance by the simple expedient of staying alive. Matt Curry didn't need to know all that, though.

"It's a good story," Curry said. "Are you sure you don't want me to print it?"

"I'm sure. I just want to hand down my decision in the morning and get on about my business. Garrison seems to be a nice enough town, but I'd just as soon be moving on."

"Well, all right. I tried to convince you." The young man grinned. "But thanks for talking to me anyway, Judge. And speaking of that court decision, have you made up your mind yet?"

Stark returned the grin and slapped the youngster on the shoulder. "Nice try, Matt," he said. "Now get out of here 'fore I take a boot to your rear end."

Curry left just as a Mexican woman from the kitchen arrived with Stark's lunch: a bowl of thick beef and chili pepper stew, beans, corn bread, and peach pie. That kept Stark happily busy for a while.

He took supper in his room, too—steak and potatoes, corn on the cob, biscuits, and more of that delicious peach cobbler. Matt Curry's visit had brought back a lot of memories, both good and bad, and Stark had spent the afternoon brooding over them as well as the Espina case. A large part of him—the part that had spent years in a simpler, more straightforward life—wanted to rule against Juan Espina's claim purely on the basis of fairness. The other part, the part dedicated to the law, knew he couldn't do that.

But maybe there was some sort of compromise he could work out. Stark spent the evening pondering that and turned in early, his thoughts still not completely clear in his head.

Not surprisingly, he didn't sleep well. He was restless, tossing and turning in the too-soft bed.

But he probably would have heard the noise outside his window anyway. Plenty of times in the past, his life had depended on his being a light sleeper, and old habits were hard to break.

He came awake cleanly, his eyes open, his senses alert. Something had disturbed him, but he didn't know what. Then it came again, a faint noise from the balcony that ran along the front of the hotel on the second story. A set of fire stairs at the end of the balcony allowed easy access to all the windows, which was one reason Stark had made sure his window was locked.

Maybe somebody was sneaking in or out of one of the other rooms, Stark thought. A lover's rendezvous, maybe. The fact that somebody was skulking around out there didn't necessarily have anything to do with him.

But he didn't believe that for a second. Every instinct in his body was crying out otherwise.

A moment later he heard a quiet scratching at the window and turned his head enough to see a shape looming there, a deeper patch of darkness against the night outside. He slid his hand toward the edge of the bed, toward the butt of the holstered LeMat that was lying on the small bedside table. If whoever was on the balcony intended to assassinate him, the son of a buck was in for a big surprise.

The skulker wanted to get into the room, however. That quickly became obvious as he worked at the window latch. He was good at what he was doing, too, Stark noted, because only a couple of minutes passed before the window slid up slowly and noiselessly.

Stark's hand closed over the butt of the LeMat. He was moving slowly and carefully himself, keeping his breathing regular so that the intruder would think he was still asleep. Through slitted eyes he watched as the man swung a leg over the windowsill and slipped into the room. The floorboards creaked slightly as he made his way through the darkness toward the bureau where Stark's saddlebags and other gear were lying.

The land grant. The man had to be after those old parchment sheets that had unexpectedly become so valuable.

Stark sat up in bed, aimed the LeMat, and said, "Looking for something, mister?"

He hoped that surprise would freeze the intruder, but instead the man let out a curse and whirled around. The man must have had his gun out already, because a tongue of flame geysered in the darkness, and a deafening report slammed into Stark's ears. He squeezed off a shot of his own as he threw himself to the side, out of the bed.

He didn't know if his bullet had found its target or not. The intruder's hurried shot had missed him. He wound up on the far side of the bed from the man, who now flung himself back toward the open window. Stark caught a glimpse of something flapping in the man's other hand and knew the varmint had gotten hold of his saddlebags.

The land grant documents were in there, Stark recalled. He had put them there before retiring for the night. Now they were on their way out the window with the nervy bastard who had broken into his room. Stark snapped another shot at the fleeing intruder, but the .41-caliber slug only chewed splinters from the window frame a couple of inches from the man's head.

With an angry curse Stark clambered to his feet and headed toward the window. He was wearing summer-weight long underwear and figured he was going to look ludicrous as all hell chasing the thief like that, but he had no choice. He couldn't let the man get away with those papers.

The intruder had disappeared, and Stark could hear his rapid footsteps as he ran along the balcony. Stark stuck his head and shoulders out the window. In the dim light coming from the hotel's downstairs windows, he spotted the shape hurrying toward the fire stairs and pivoted the striker on the LeMat's hammer down so that it would detonate the shotgun shell in the lower barrel. The intruder was almost at the other end of the balcony, so Stark had to hurry his shot. The LeMat boomed like thunder as the shotgun shell exploded and sent a charge of buckshot whistling along the balcony. The man stumbled and caught himself, but Stark saw the saddlebags fall from his hand. He wouldn't get away with those papers, anyway.

That wasn't enough to satisfy Stark. He wanted to capture the thief so that he could question him and find out who had hired him to steal the documents. Stark climbed through the window and pounded along the balcony in his stocking feet as his quarry fled down the fire stairs, moving more slowly and more clumsily now because of the buckshot that had peppered him.

"Hold it, mister!" Stark yelled when he reached the top of the stairs. The thief, almost at the bottom, twisted around and fired again, and the slug whined past Stark's head. Instinctively Stark triggered off a return shot.

The man cried out in pain and doubled over. Grimacing, Stark breathed a fervent, "Damn it!" He hadn't meant to wound the man seriously; he had intended only to shoot a leg out from under him, but his quick reaction and the fact that he was aiming downhill had made the bullet go higher—right into the man's belly, from the looks of it.

Folks were yelling, and lights were coming on all over town. The shooting had drawn plenty of attention. Stark backtracked a couple of steps and picked up the saddlebags the thief had dropped. Then he clattered down the fire stairs, covering the huddled shape at the bottom as he approached. The man no longer seemed to be a threat, though. He was curled up in a ball of agony. Low whimpers of pain escaped from his throat.

Somebody came running up, and Stark recognized Sheriff Higgins's voice as the lawman bellowed, "What in blue blazes is goin' on?"

"It's Judge Stark, Sheriff," Stark told him.

"Judge Stark's been shot?" Higgins asked.

"No, *I'm* Judge Stark. I shot this fella."

"What for?"

"He was trying to steal those land grant papers," Stark explained. "Can we get some light over here?"

Bystanders were crowding around now. Higgins told one of them to run into the hotel and fetch a lamp. The man did so, bringing back a kerosene lantern that he held high over his head so that it cast a large circle of yellow light over the scene. Stark was acutely aware that he was standing there in his long underwear, saddlebags draped over his left shoulder, a smoking gun in his right hand. He probably looked mighty comical, he thought, but there was nothing he could do about that now.

The wounded man had stopped writhing and moaning.

"Turn him over," Stark told Sheriff Higgins. "I want to take a look at him."

The sheriff grasped the man's shoulders and hauled him around onto his back. The man's head lolled loosely on his neck, and Stark bit back a curse. Glassy eyes stared lifelessly from a lean, hard-bitten, beard-stubbled face.

Stark had never seen the dead man before.

"You know him?" he asked Higgins.

The lawman shook his head. "Can't say as I do. 'Course, there's fellas driftin' in and out of here all the time. Chuck line riders and the like."

The dead man was no fiddle-footed cowboy, Stark decided. More likely a hardcase on the dodge from a crime somewhere else. Stark addressed the crowd. "Anybody seen this man before?"

The sight was not a pretty one. The man's face was twisted in death, and the front of his ragged shirt was sodden with blood. But the onlookers crowded around to study the corpse, and after a moment one man said, "I don't know his name, Judge, but I seen him around town the past couple of days. Stayed in the saloons most of the time, he did, and he done plenty of drinkin'."

"You talk to him?" Stark asked.

The man shook his head. "No, sir, I never did. I generally steer clear of gun-hung gents like that."

"Probably a smart thing to do," Stark grunted. He would likely never know the dead man's name, but it was easy enough to figure out what sort of hombre he'd been. He wouldn't care what sort of job he was hired to do, as long as it paid well—even sneaking into the hotel room of a federal circuit court judge and stealing important evidence.

Without the original documents, any ruling Stark made on the land grant issue would probably be thrown out in an appellate court. Stark knew that.

Travis Richmond and Ben Tompkins had to be aware of that, too.

He sighed. There was no use speculating. A dead man could not testify, and nothing could be proven against either of the ranchers or their lawyer, Alfred Fanning—although, Stark thought grimly, this was the sort of stunt he might expect Fanning to pull.

"You can take care of this, Sheriff," he told Higgins. "I don't figure anyone will claim the body. The county'll probably wind up burying him."

"Reckon we can find room in the graveyard. You ain't hurt, are you, Judge?"

Stark shook his head. "Only my dignity, and I never had a whole hell of a lot of that in the first place. I'm going back upstairs."

"You want me to have a deputy keep an eye on your room?"

The Diablo Grant

"I don't think anybody'll bother me again tonight." Stark looked down at the body of the man he had killed. "Not after the welcome this unlucky son of a bitch got."

There were mutters of agreement from the crowd. Stark had demonstrated vividly that he could do more than wield a gavel.

He turned, went up the stairs, and returned to his room. Despite his weariness, he didn't figure he would sleep much the rest of the night.

He was right about that, too.

Chapter Six

If anything, the town hall and the street outside were even more crowded the next morning. Stark didn't try to force his way through the mob; he went in the back door, as he had left the day before. He was wearing the same sober black suit he usually wore for court, but today the shell belt with the holstered LeMat was strapped around his hips.

He wasn't going into that courtroom unarmed. Not with what he had to say.

As he came up to the table that served as his bench, he scanned the crowd. Silence spread through the room as they looked back at him, knowing that he held the future of many of them in his hands. Behind the table where Richmond and Tompkins were sitting with Fanning, the other cattlemen from the Diablo Valley had taken their places. Cowboys and townsmen were about

The Diablo Grant

equally mixed in the rest of the room, but all of them had a stake in this case. To a large extent Garrison depended for its survival on the ranches in Diablo Valley; without them the town might not survive. In the long run the economy of the entire territory would be affected by the decision Stark would render here.

The scattering of Mexican farmers who had attended the day before to support Juan in his claim were nowhere to be seen today. Stark guessed that the cowboys had refused to let them in and had probably run them off.

Except for Billy Chadwick, Matt Curry, and Don Alfonso Montoya, Juan had no allies here today. But those three—*and* the fact that he had the law on his side—were enough.

Stark took off his hat, placed it on the table, and picked up the gavel. Sheriff Higgins, waiting to one side, shouted for everyone to stand. After he had called the court to order, Stark settled in his chair and banged the gavel on the table. The spectators sat down and waited in tense silence.

"We're here today to determine the legality of the Espina land grant and the ownership of Diablo Valley," Stark said, well aware that everybody in the room knew that already but wanting to make sure everything was on the record. "I've heard the testimony and examined the evidence in this case—although there was an attempt last night to steal and probably destroy that evidence." He wasn't telling the crowd anything new there, either; the story of the shoot-out on the hotel balcony was no doubt all over town before breakfast was over.

Stark continued, "This case is both very complicated

and very simple: complicated in terms of how it will affect the people involved, but simple in terms of the law." No point in putting it off, he told himself. He took a deep breath. "I find that the Espina land grant is legal and binding, under the terms of the Treaty of Guadalupe Hidalgo—"

He couldn't go on, couldn't make himself heard over the roar of anger and disbelief that exploded in the town hall. It had begun before the words were out of his mouth, as soon as the spectators realized that he was ruling in favor of Juan Espina's claim. They were on their feet, shouting and cursing and glaring at him.

Juan looked terrified as the wave of noise and resentment washed over him. Billy Chadwick slipped an arm around the old man's bony shoulders to reassure him.

Stark picked up the gavel and pounded on the table as hard and as fast as he could. He had more to say, and he was determined to say it. Sheriff Higgins was yelling for quiet but being ignored. Finally, after several minutess, the tumult died down enough for Stark's gavel-pounding to be heard, and the noise gradually subsided so that Stark could proceed.

"I find the land grant legal and binding," he repeated, almost shouting now, "and I find that Juan Espina is the rightful owner of Diablo Valley! However, there are other issues to be considered!"

That caught the spectators' attention and prompted them to quiet down a little more. Some even sat down again to hear what else Stark had to say.

In a more normal tone of voice, he went on, "I also find that since the settlers who are currently living in Diablo Valley acquired their land in good faith, they

The Diablo Grant

are entitled to compensation for any loss they may incur as a result of this ruling."

Alfred Fanning shot to his feet. "What sort of compensation, Your Honor?" Beside him, both Richmond and Tompkins looked angry and defiant.

"Under the law, improvements such as buildings, fences, et cetera, are considered part of the property in question—real property, so to speak. Possessions are not. So all the livestock, equipment, furnishings, and such-like belonging to Mr. Richmond, Mr. Tompkins, and the other ranchers in Diablo Valley will remain their property."

Travis Richmond demanded, "What good are cattle without grass and water?"

Ben Tompkins added, "I built my ranch house with my own hands, damn it! And now you're sayin' it belongs to that filthy Meskin!"

Stark hammered with the gavel as others in the audience shouted at him. "That's the law, blast it!" he said, raising his voice again. "I didn't write it, but by God I intend to enforce it!"

A husky young blond man standing behind the ranchers' table yelled, "You won't get away with this, you son of a bitch!"

Stark was about to declare the young man in contempt of court when he went on, "That old man will die before we let him take over Diablo Valley!"

Stark slammed the gavel down as he came to his feet, filled now with anger of his own. "I won't have anybody making threats in my court!" he bellowed. "Who are you, sir?"

Richmond had turned and was holding on tightly to the young man's shoulder, and Stark could see the family resemblance now. He wasn't surprised when Richmond said, "He's my son Cord, Your Honor. And he's upset by this ruling, as all of us are."

"I still won't allow threats in my court." Stark turned to Higgins. "Sheriff, take that young man into custody and hold him until he cools off."

Higgins glanced at Stark. "Uh, Judge, are you right sure—"

Stark was stubborn enough not to back down once he had issued the order, but in the next instant none of that mattered anymore. Cord Richmond pulled away from his father, howling, "I'll kill the old bastard myself!". Then he flung himself at Juan Espina.

"Stop him, Sheriff!" Stark yelled. Higgins was already moving, but he wasn't fast enough to keep Cord from reaching the other table. The young firebrand lunged at the horrified Juan Espina, hands outstretched to grasp the scrawny neck and snap it like a twig.

Billy Chadwick got in Cord's way, surging up out of his chair and hooking a punch to the young man's stomach. That slowed Cord down, but not enough to keep him from barreling into Chadwick. The lawyer went down under the rush of the bigger, younger man.

Higgins reached Cord then and grabbed his shoulder. As he hauled Cord around, a cowboy leaped on Higgins's back and let out a rebel yell. Punchers from Antlers, the Box BT, and the other spreads in Diablo Valley surged forward in a yelling, outraged tide, sweeping over the tables. In a matter of seconds the town hall was filled with pandemonium. Fists and curses clogged the air. Sheriff Higgins and the handful of deputies in the room tried to restore order, but it was hopeless.

Several cowhands started toward Stark, eager to take

The Diablo Grant

out their anger on the person they considered the source of their troubles, but they stopped in their tracks as he came up out of his chair and palmed the LeMat from its holster. He squeezed the trigger, sending the charge of buckshot from the shotgun shell into the ceiling over the heads of the rioters.

The thunderous blast of the LeMat was enough to shock the howling cowboys into silence. Stark thumbed back the hammer as he lowered the gun and warned, "I'll shoot the next man who throws a punch! Back off! Back off, damn it!"

Even though he was outnumbered a hundred to one—and most of those hundred were packing iron of their own—he moved the crowd back by sheer force of will as he came out from behind the table and hurried over to where he had last seen Chadwick, Juan, and Higgins. The old man was huddled under the smaller table, Stark saw to his relief, and the sheriff and the attorney were both all right, too, if a little the worse for wear. Both men sported fresh bruises and cuts from the flailing fists they had encountered in the melee.

"Tompkins! Richmond!" Stark's voice crackled with anger. "I reckon most of these boys work for you. Call 'em off now and get 'em out of town! I can call in the army if I have to to settle down this ruckus, and if I do, some of you won't see the light of day for a damned long time!"

"You heard him, men," Travis Richmond said. "Back off. Get out of here and go back to the ranch."

"But, boss," a gangling cowpoke protested, "he said that weren't our ranch no more!"

Another cowboy added, "And he said Cord was under arrest!"

Cord Richmond was standing beside his father, blood

dripping from his nose where he had taken a punch, from Higgins or Chadwick or one of his own compadres by accident. He wiped the back of his hand across his nose, leaving a crimson smear on his cheek. "I don't give a damn," he said. "I'll go to jail. I'll hang if it means that old drunk won't get our ranch!"

"Shut up, Cord," Richmond snapped. The rancher looked at Stark and went on, "I can get these boys out of here easier if Cord goes with them, Judge."

"Take him," Stark said disgustedly. "Take him and get out, all of you. And you'd damn well better keep him on a tight rein, Richmond, him and all those other riders of yours. Same goes for you, Tompkins."

"What about our ranches?" Tompkins demanded. "What happens now?"

Stark took a deep breath. "I reckon we ought to all cool off a mite. Then we'll sit down and work out the details without all this fussing. I'll let you know when." He raised his voice. "In case you ain't figured it out, this court's adjourned!"

He stood there, gun in hand, while the still-angry cowhands were prodded out of the hall by their bosses. Cord Richmond was still casting murderous glances at Juan when his father shoved him roughly out the door. The townspeople left, too, spilling out into the street to talk angrily among themselves. Although they had not reacted with violence to Stark's ruling, the way the cowboys had, Stark knew they were just as unhappy with the outcome of the hearing.

When the room was almost empty, Stark finally holstered the LeMat and went over to Billy Chadwick. The lawyer worked his jaw back and forth and grinned wryly. "It's not broken," he said, "but it feels like a mule kicked it." His expression turning more serious, he went on, "You know this isn't over, don't you, Judge?"

"Yeah, I know," Stark said.

Don Alfonso Montoya came up to him. "You reached the proper decision, Judge Stark," he said. "That took great courage."

"Either that or a hard head," Stark grunted. "Where's your daughter? She didn't get caught in the middle of that ruckus, did she?"

"I had one of my men take her out of the hall as soon as I saw that things might turn unpleasant. I must find her now and make certain she is all right, but I wanted to tell you first that I respect your judgment, Your Honor."

"I decided the way you and President Díaz wanted, I reckon. But that wasn't why I did it," Stark said coolly.

"*Sí*. This I know." Montoya inclined his head for a second, then hurried out in search of his daughter.

Matt Curry was standing nearby, his clothes somewhat disheveled and a shiner beginning to form around his right eye. That didn't stop him from scribbling furiously on his ever-present pad of paper, however. Without looking up, he said, "This is really something, Judge Stark. This story is bound to make the papers back east!"

Stark felt like giving the youngster a good, swift boot in the pants. The judge had just played hob with the lives of hundreds of people and turned things upside down in this section of the territory—and to Curry it was just a story that might impress his father. But Stark's quick surge of anger quickly evaporated. He couldn't fault Curry for being dedicated to his profession. After all, it was Stark's own dedication to *his* job that had led him to rule as he had, even though by instinct and background he was more inclined to side with the ranchers.

"Glad I could help, son," he said dryly to Curry, then turned to Chadwick. "You'd better keep a closer eye than ever on Juan now. There are a few hundred people out there with a grudge against him."

Chadwick nodded. "I intend to."

For the first time, Juan spoke up. "But this—this is not my fault," he said miserably. "Why is everyone so angry at me?"

There was no way to explain it to him, not after all the years of tequila that had clouded his brain, Stark thought. He settled for putting a hand on the old man's shoulder and saying, "Don't worry, Juan. It's going to be all right. The law's on your side."

But Stark had to wonder now if, after all, that was going to be enough.

Excitement was still coursing through Matt Curry's veins when he got back to the office of the *Territorial Observer* a little later. Things had worked out even better than he had dared to hope when the issue of the land grant first came up. Not only had Juan Espina's claim been upheld, but the judge in the case was the colorful Earl Stark. Even though Stark had declined to discuss his background, enough of it was a matter of public record so that Matt could let his readers know what an interesting individual the judge was.

The real story was the land grant, of course. Matt went directly to his desk, pulled a fresh pad of paper

The Diablo Grant

in front of him, and went to work composing a story out of the rough notes he had scribbled in the town hall. He was barely aware of time passing as he worked, just as he paid no attention to the bruises and aches and black eye he had picked up during the brief riot following Judge Stark's announcement of the verdict. Matt was lost in the words flowing from his pencil to the paper.

When he was finished, he read back over what he had written, made a few changes, then started setting the type for the story, which would go smack-dab in the middle of the front page of the next edition. His assistants would be in tonight to help him with the printing press, and tomorrow morning the paper would be on the streets, carrying the news of the dramatic events at the town hall for all to read.

Of course, a part of Matt's brain reminded him, nearly everybody in town had actually *been* there to witness the whole scene for themselves. But that didn't really matter. This special issue of the *Observer* would doubtless be distributed far and wide, all through the territory and maybe even in Texas. Then the news services that covered the world by telegraph would pick up the story, and he would be well on his way to being famous, just as famous as his father.

He had the front page composed and locked in and the press ready to go when a voice—a female voice—said from the doorway, "Señor Curry?"

Still a little dopey from the work on which he had been concentrating for so long, Matt looked up and saw a lovely young Mexican woman standing just inside the office, a slightly quizzical expression on her beautiful face.

"Señorita Montoya?" he said, recognizing her as the daughter of the diplomat sent by President Porfirio Díaz. "What can I do for you?"

"There was something I hoped I could do for you," she said with a smile. She lifted the folded newspaper she held in her hand. "I was just reading your last edition of the *Observer*."

Matt flushed, pleased that such an attractive woman had been reading his work. She spoke English with only a faint trace of an accent, and he had no doubt that she could handle the written language just as well. As the daughter of a Mexican aristocrat, she might even have been educated in the United States.

"I hope you like what you read in there," he told her, gesturing at the paper in her hand.

"Very much. Journalism is one of my interests, and your paper is well written. There were just a few things that concerned me."

Matt's spirits, which had been bounding high, suddenly plummeted. Angelina Montoya had found things in the paper—*his* paper—that she didn't like.

"What are they?" he asked as he crossed the room toward her. He was aware that he was wearing a heavy leather apron and probably had ink smeared on his hands and face, but he didn't care. If she had found mistakes in the paper, he had to know about them.

She looked and sounded somewhat hesitant as she said, "There are words that are not spelled correctly. Not many of them, but enough to be distracting to someone such as myself."

Matt felt as if he'd been kicked in the stomach. Typographical errors! They had always been the bane of his existence. His brief stint on the staff of one of his

The Diablo Grant

father's papers had been marred by them. But as he got carried away in the emotions of the stories he wrote, the mistakes inevitably crept in. And while he could catch them in someone else's copy, he rarely saw them in his own.

"I'm sorry," he told Angelina miserably. "I have trouble with that."

"Would you like me to help you?" she offered. "My journalism professors at the university always praised my skills as a proofreader."

"You studied journalism?" he asked, unable to contain his surprise. He had figured she might've gone to some finishing school back east—but a university? And as a journalism student, at that?

"*Sí.*" She smiled. "One of many things I have done that my father opposed. I greatly admire Miss Elizabeth Cochrane and wish to be like her."

"Elizabeth Cochrane—you mean Nellie Bly!"

Angelina nodded. "*Sí.* Nellie Bly. I wish to write of injustices in my country, just as she does in the New York *World.*"

Matt let out a low whistle. The young woman who had adopted the name Nellie Bly for her newspaper work had been a reporter for only a year or so, but already she was famous. Evidently her fame had reached all the way to Mexico City, to another young, attractive woman, this one named Angelina Montoya.

"Well, you've certainly set your sights high," Matt told her. "But I reckon you'll make it if you want to badly enough."

Angelina held up the paper again. "Would you like me to read the copy for your next issue?"

Matt shook his head ruefully. "It's already all set in

type, and my helpers will be here after a while—" He broke off as he looked past Angelina at the dusk gathering in the street outside. It was much later than he had thought; he had been so caught up in his work that he hadn't noticed that the day was almost gone. "Well, they'll be here any minute, I imagine," he went on. "But I'd like to see the mistakes in last week's paper, if you don't mind pointing them out."

"Of course," she said. She started to unfold the paper. "You can see—"

Matt took a chance and interrupted her. "Why don't we do this over dinner?" he suggested. "There's a good restaurant right down the street, if you think your father wouldn't mind."

"I am a grown woman," she said rather tartly. "I do not have to have my father's permission to have dinner with a man . . . although he may perhaps be somewhat scandalized. He does not yet realize that these are modern times."

She was certainly different from all the rich young Mexican women he had seen, Matt thought. None of them would have been so forward as to come here to the office and talk to him alone like this; in fact, they wouldn't have been allowed to go anywhere without some hefty old *mamacita* along to serve as *dueña*. But evidently Angelina went where she wanted and didn't worry about being accompanied by a chaperone. She had probably rebelled at the very notion. Matt had a hunch Don Alfonso had his hands full with such a strong-willed daughter who had interests that would not be considered seemly or proper below the border.

Matt was glad she was here in Garrison. A young woman who was beautiful, and smart, and interested in the same things he was . . . Well, he was no fool. He wasn't going to waste this opportunity to get to know Angelina Montoya better.

He whipped off his apron, picked up a rag, and wiped ink from his hands. "Any on my face?" he asked Angelina.

She shook her head with a smile, and Matt reached for his coat. He shrugged into it, offered her his arm, and led her out of the office. His assistants could handle the printing themselves, and anyway he would be back in plenty of time to make sure everything was going all right.

He hoped Don Alfonso wasn't the type to send some of those *federales* after him once he found out what was going on. You never could tell about hotheaded hidalgos like that, especially where their daughters were concerned.

But Matt had a feeling that Angelina just might be worth the risk. As she walked beside him in the twilight, the delicate yet heady scent of the perfume in her thick, lustrous hair filling his nostrils, he found himself thinking about something besides ink and paper and type for a change.

It was a good feeling.

And for now at least, he had completely forgotten about Juan Espina.

Chapter Seven

Stark slept late the next morning—catching up on the rest that had been disturbed the night before, he supposed. He went downstairs after nine o'clock, picked up a copy of the *Territorial Observer* from the front desk, and had breakfast in the hotel dining room. As he ate he scanned the story by Matt Curry that took up most of the front page. The large headline read: JUDGE RULES FOR ESPINA IN LAND GRANT CASE. By this time everybody in town knew what had happened and who was responsible for it. Judging by the way the other diners were studying him, he guessed that most folks were not too happy with him.

After breakfast he strolled through the lobby to the boardwalk along Garrison's main street. Pedestrians on the boardwalk and riders on horseback all seemed to be staring at him, too. That came as no surprise. He

The Diablo Grant

was the man who had totally disrupted all their lives by ruling in favor of Juan Espina.

But Stark had come up with what he thought was an equitable plan to handle the transfer of ownership of Diablo Valley, and maybe once people had heard all the details, they would see things differently.

He tried to ignore the hostile stares as he started across the street toward Billy Chadwick's office. He wanted to have a long talk with the lawyer, and as unpleasant as the idea was, he knew he would have to talk to Alfred Fanning, too, along with Richmond and Tompkins.

Before Stark could reach the opposite boardwalk, he had to stop to let a fancy buggy pulled by a team of fine, high-stepping black horses move past him. His eyes widened in surprise when he caught a glimpse of the buggy's occupant. Juan Espina sat there in expensive finery to match the buggy and the team, and beside him was a young woman in a brightly colored silk gown. Juan was handling the team. His face was set in a disdainful sneer for the people he passed. He didn't seem to notice Stark.

"What in the name of blue-footed horned toads?" Stark muttered to himself. Juan seemed to have been transformed overnight from a cowering, confused old man into an arrogant dandy. As Stark watched, the buggy rolled down the street and pulled up in front of a ladies' dress shop. Juan got down, helped the young woman with him to disembark, and took her arm to lead her into the shop.

The citizens of Garrison might have given Stark some dirty looks earlier, but they regarded Juan and his companion with downright hostility. Stark didn't like the looks of this, and he hurried on to Billy Chadwick's office to see if the lawyer knew anything about the changes in Juan.

He went up the stairs to Chadwick's office and opened the door without knocking. The lawyer turned away from the window overlooking the main street, where he couldn't have failed to notice Juan and the young woman drive by in the fancy buggy. "I saw you coming," he said to Stark, "and I reckon I know why you're here."

"What's happened to Juan?" Stark demanded. "He looks like a different person than the one he was yesterday, and I'm not sure I like the change."

Chadwick sighed wearily and went behind his desk to sit down. He gestured Stark toward the leather chair in front of the desk. "I'm afraid Juan's had a serious attack of sudden-riches disease. He seemed to wake up yesterday afternoon and realize he was a wealthy man. He started buying things then, and he hasn't stopped yet."

"Wait just a darned minute," Stark protested. "That old man doesn't have a bit more cash today than he did before my ruling in court."

"I know that, and so do you. So do all the folks here in town, for that matter. But Juan's a land tycoon now, and people figure he'll have plenty of money in the future."

"So they're selling to him on credit." Stark suppressed a groan of frustration.

"And Juan's buying, hand over fist," Chadwick said with a nod. "Don't get me wrong; the town hates the ruling you handed down, and I reckon they hate you and me and maybe even young Matt Curry for being part of it. But business is business, and if Juan's going to own the whole blasted Diablo Valley, most people in this town want him for a customer."

Stark sat back in the leather chair, shook his head, and grunted, "Don't reckon I can blame 'em for that. Who's the girl I saw with him?"

"Her name's Dolores. If she's got a last name, I don't think I've ever heard it. She's, ah, she works over in the red-light district—or did, until now, that is."

"Why, that old goat!" Stark exclaimed. "He gets himself a little money—the *promise* of a little money—and he goes out and hires his own personal trollop!"

Chadwick shook his head. "No, I don't think it's like that. Matt told me that Dolores was with him the night he found those land grant papers in Juan's shack."

"What? That didn't come out at the trial!"

"Juan and Matt both asked me not to mention that part of it, since it wasn't really relevant." Chadwick shrugged. "Evidently Dolores has been looking out after Juan for a long time, helping him home when he's drunk, making sure nothing happens to him when he's passed out, that sort of thing. I don't think the old-timer takes any, ah, romantic interest in her. But now that it appears he's going to be wealthy, Juan wants to take care of her the way she's been taking care of him."

"So he buys her pretty dresses and drives her around town in a fancy buggy so people can look at her and see that she's a lady after all," Stark mused. "Surely he knows that's not going to work. Folks won't really change their opinion of her, even if they pretend to."

"Just like they still think he's a dirty old drunk. Sure, I think Juan understands that, at least deep down. But he's never had anything, Judge, never known what it's like for people to even pretend to respect him. For Juan, that's enough. It's more than enough. It's gone to his head." Chadwick sighed. "He's stopped listening to my advice. I don't reckon I can control him anymore. Hell, maybe I don't even have the right to try."

"Trying to help somebody isn't the same as controlling him," Stark pointed out. He put his hands on his knees and pushed himself to his feet. "I don't mind telling you, Billy, this worries me. Everything's changed for Juan, and he's not going to be able to handle it by himself."

"I'll do what I can," Chadwick promised. "But I don't know if it's going to do any good."

"Maybe once Juan hears what I've got in mind for that valley, he'll settle down again. I figure we'll have that meeting tonight. I want you and Juan there, of course, and I'm going to tell Richmond and Tompkins and Fanning to be there, too."

"How about letting me in on what you have in mind?" Chadwick asked.

Stark thought it over, then shook his head. "I'm still ironing out all the details. Why don't we get together this afternoon, though, before the other meeting, and I can fill you in then. The leading citizens in the town need to be there, too, so they'll know what to expect."

Chadwick nodded. "All right. I'll round up the mayor and the town council, along with a few of the other important folks around here. I figure some of them will have a few complaints."

"That's why I want this meeting with them," Stark said. "We'll hash it all out first, and then this evening, when Juan comes face to face with Richmond and Tompkins, we'll have everything already worked out with the town. If we're lucky, that'll save some time and hard feelings."

"So you don't want Juan at the first meeting?"

"No, not him or those cattlemen. They'd just muddy the waters."

"They *do* have more at stake than anybody else," Chadwick pointed out.

"And they're hotheaded, too. No, I want everything squared away so that they don't have as much to argue about." Stark rubbed his bearded jaw. "Wouldn't take much to make this whole town blow sky-high. But we're going to pull the fuse on that case of dynamite, Counselor."

"I just hope the fuse isn't too short," Chadwick said grimly.

"So do I," Stark agreed with a sigh. "So do I."

When Stark got back to his hotel, the fancy buggy and fine black horses were tied to the hitchrack outside. He frowned, knowing what that was likely to mean. When he went inside, he saw that he was right.

Juan Espina was standing at the desk, the lush young woman called Dolores beside him. As the flustered clerk tried to make excuses, Juan said loudly and angrily, "I tell you, I want the finest rooms you have, señor!"

Stark moved up to the desk. "What's the problem?" he asked.

"Oh, there you are, Judge Stark!" the clerk exclaimed. "This, ah, gentleman wants to rent rooms here for himself and the, ah, young lady, but I've tried to explain to him that nothing is available. Perhaps you could—"

Stark looked pointedly at the keys hanging on the board behind the desk and suggested, "Why don't you put them in twelve and fourteen? Those rooms adjoin, and I happen to know they're empty." The rooms were across the hall from Stark's.

"But, Your Honor—" the clerk objected.

"Now, just go ahead and register them, son," Stark said firmly. "That's better than starting a big ruckus right here in your lobby, isn't it?"

"Well . . . I suppose so. But as payment—"

Again Stark interrupted. "As long as guests have bags, you let them pay when they leave, right?" He gestured at the parcels stacked on the floor next to Juan and Dolores. "There are plenty of bags here, and I saw more in that buggy parked outside. So I reckon you'd better let these folks register and have somebody help them take their belongings up to their rooms."

The clerk nodded wearily and said, "Of course, Judge. If that's what you want, I'll be glad to." He turned the register around and told Juan, "You'll have to sign in."

His dignity restored, Juan picked up the pen, dipped it in the inkwell, and signed his name in wavering, spidery script. "I was taught to write by the padres at the mission, many years ago," he told Stark proudly.

"That's good," Stark said. "Let me give you a hand with your possibles, Juan."

There were at least a dozen people in the hotel lobby, which meant it wouldn't take long for the news of this latest development in Juan Espina's life to be spread all over town. Stark had his own reasons for interceding on the old man's behalf. If Juan was letting his newfound prosperity affect him as much as Chadwick had described, then Stark wanted the old-timer somewhere close by, so that he could keep an eye on him. Besides, with so many new enemies, Juan might be safer here in the hotel than in the shack he had always called home.

Stark got Juan and Dolores settled in the two adjoining rooms, which, although furnished in a style typical of respectable cattletown hotels, must have seemed like the lap of luxury to the old man and the young woman. He left Juan staring in amazement at the big four-poster bed with its feather mattress and went back to his own room, catty-cornered across the hall.

Billy Chadwick came by the hotel a little later to tell Stark that the preliminary meeting with Garrison's civic leaders was set for two o'clock in the lawyer's office. "It'll be a mite crowded with all of us in there," Chadwick said, "but I got the idea you wanted this kept sort of quiet for the time being."

"That's right," Stark agreed. "Did you tell anybody what it's about?"

"Nope, just that you wanted to see them." Chadwick chuckled. "To tell you the truth, Judge, I think some of these ol' boys want to give you a piece of their mind. They're not happy about everything that's happened."

"Neither am I," Stark admitted. "But the law is the law, and sometimes we've just got to make the best of it."

When Chadwick had gone, Stark sat on the bed and opened his saddlebags to take out what he needed to clean the LeMat, the Winchester, and his old greener. Back in the days when he was still studying the law, he had spent many an hour with one of the law books he'd found propped open in his lap, reading and pondering while he cleaned his guns. He had found that giving his hands something to do, some well-practiced chore, seemed to make his mind work more efficiently. That was still true.

As he worked with the rags and oil and cleaning rod, he thought about the plan he had worked out. There was no question that Juan Espina was not qualified in any way, shape, or fashion to run the ranches of Diablo Valley. That was a chore best handled by the men who had built those ranches: Travis Richmond, Ben Tompkins, and all the cattlemen who owned smaller spreads. What was needed was some sort of lease arrangement whereby the ranches and the men who ran them would not be disturbed. In return, Juan would receive a share of the profits from Antlers, the Boxed BT, and the other spreads. Even a small percentage would make the old man far richer than he could have ever dreamed of being. Stark had a feeling Juan would go for the deal. There was really nothing else he could do. Richmond and Tompkins might balk at sharing any of their profits with the old Mexican, but in the end they would have no choice, either. No one would be completely satisfied, but at least it was an arrangement they could all live with, Stark believed.

He ate a leisurely lunch in the hotel dining room, then ambled over to Billy Chadwick's office. Although it wasn't two o'clock yet, several of the men whose presence Stark had requested were already there. Chadwick introduced him to Edmund Wells, the mayor of Garrison and the owner of the town's bank, and to the other members of the town council, all of them local businessmen. Several other townsmen were there as well, and Stark knew that some of them had already extended credit to Juan Espina. They might be here to complain about the old man's sudden reversal of fortune, but they weren't above taking advantage of it.

When Chadwick indicated that everyone was present, Stark raised his voice and said, "Thank you for coming, gentlemen. The reason I asked you here today is to explain to you what I have in mind regarding Juan Espina and the Diablo Valley."

"You mean there's *more*, Judge Stark?" Edmund Wells asked sharply. "This business has already ruined two of the finest men I know, Travis Richmond and Ben Tompkins."

Two of his finest *customers* was what Wells meant, Stark thought as the other men murmured in agreement. He held up his hands to quiet them down and said, "I didn't come to Garrison to ruin anybody. But it's my job to interpret the law as I see fit, and that's exactly what I did. Anybody who wants to take issue with that can take it up with the attorney general and the Justice Department."

No one challenged him, and after a moment he went on, "Just because that land grant is legal and binding doesn't mean everything has to be turned on its head around here. Nobody wants to uproot Richmond and Tompkins and those other ranchers from their land."

"It's not their land anymore," one of the councilmen pointed out. "You said it belongs to Juan Espina, Judge."

"Officially it does," Stark admitted. "But Juan's no rancher, and we all know it. What I have in mind is an arrangement whereby Richmond and Tompkins and the others can keep their spreads and go on just as they have, in return for paying a percentage of their profits to Juan for leasing the land."

That announcement brought another round of muttering, and this time Stark let it run its course. Finally Wells said, "I don't know if Trav and Ben will go along with an agreement like that."

"They really have no other choice—" Stark began.

Before he could finish his explanation, the door of Chadwick's office was suddenly thrown open. It slammed back against the wall behind it, making the men at the meeting jump in surprise. Instinctively Stark's hand went to his revolver, and he saw Chadwick reacting the same way. Old habits died hard—especially the ones that kept a man from dying the same way.

But the newcomer was no threat. In fact, swaying back and forth in the doorway, he looked as if he could barely stay on his feet. Juan Espina's ruffled silk shirt and short charro jacket were disheveled, and the flat-crowned hat on his grizzled head was cocked at a disreputable angle. Tufts of white hair stuck out wildly from beneath it. A nearly empty bottle of tequila dangled from Juan's gnarled left hand.

"Juan!" Chadwick exclaimed as he leaped to his feet and hurried over to the old man. "What are you doing here?"

Juan drew himself up, belched, and said, "I have heard that you are meeting to decide what to do about the filthy old Mexican who is suddenly so rich."

"That's not the way it is at all, Juan," Chadwick told

him as he took hold of the man's bony left arm. "We just got together to have a talk—"

"You are plotting against me!" Juan accused shrilly. "Dolores said you would not do this thing. She said you were my friend, Señor Chadwick, and that the judge was a fair man. But both of you are here, meeting with these jackals!" A sweep of his free hand took in the townsmen in the room.

Edmund Wells jumped to his feet. "Now, see here—" he began hotly.

"Sit down, Mr. Mayor," Chadwick said. "Please. I'll handle this."

"You will not handle Juan Espina," the old man said haughtily. "I am a rich man now. I own the entire Diablo Valley! I will make my own decisions!"

Stark bit back a curse. It was bad enough that Juan had let his unexpected good luck go to his head; now he was drunk, too, and feeling his oats. Stark wondered briefly where he had gotten the tequila, then decided it didn't matter. There were dozens of cantinas and saloons in this town whose proprietors would have been glad to advance the old man the cost of a bottle.

Juan pointed a shaky finger at the townsmen and said, "Nothing will be the same here, ever again! I warn you! All those who looked down on me—all those who spat on me!—they will regret their cruelty."

"How dare you speak to us like that, you old . . . old reprobate?" Wells sputtered. A couple of his colleagues were holding him back. Chadwick was still grasping Juan's arm, ready to get between the old man and the others if trouble broke out.

"Look, Juan," Stark said, trying to reason with him,

"there's no need to get upset about any of this. We were just trying to work out a deal that you can agree to with Tompkins and Richmond."

"No deals," Juan declared. "The valley is mine. They must get out!"

"You can't mean that, Juan," Chadwick said. "That wouldn't do anyone any good."

"The valley is mine!" Juan repeated. "No deals!"

The mood in the room was getting uglier by the second, Stark sensed. He wished Juan hadn't slipped away from Dolores. From his brief meeting with the young woman, he had been able to tell that she genuinely cared for Juan. But she couldn't watch him all the time, and evidently his thirst had overcome his desire to flaunt his wealth to the townspeople. He had ended his buying spree and gone on a drinking binge instead.

Stark knew he had to put a stop to this before it got any worse. "Billy, get Juan out of here and take him back to his hotel room. Keep him there until tonight if you have to sit on him."

Chadwick nodded. "I'll get Matt Curry to help me. We'll take care of him, Judge."

"No!" Juan protested as Chadwick tried to steer him out the door. "I am a rich man! You cannot tell me what to do!"

There was a rapid patter of footsteps on the stairs outside, and Dolores appeared. "Juan!" she said scoldingly. "Where did you go? I was so worried about you."

Her arrival was a stroke of luck, Stark thought. The old man calmed down immediately, and he allowed Chadwick and Dolores to lead him back down the stairs and toward the hotel.

That left Stark facing the angry townspeople. "You heard him, Judge," Wells said. "He's not going to be reasonable."

"Let's give him some time to sober up," Stark suggested. "I reckon if he has a chance to think about it, Juan will see that he has no choice but to go along with that plan I told you about. It's the only fair thing for everybody."

One of the men said bitterly, "That old geezer doesn't care about fair. All he wants to do is even the score for the way everybody's picked on him all these years."

"He was never mistreated," Wells said. "He always had food and shelter. And God knows, he had all the liquor any man could drink!"

"And the whole town scorned him," Stark said. "I reckon that must've hurt him more than any of you ever knew."

"We didn't mean to . . . to offend him," Wells said, sounding a little sheepish now. "None of us ever dreamed that he had any feelings to hurt!"

"Anybody can be hurt," Stark said with a sigh. "Anybody."

And he hoped the town of Garrison and the ranchers of Diablo Valley weren't about to pay for that now.

Chapter Eight

Travis Richmond, Ben Tompkins, and several riders from Antlers and the Boxed BT rode into town after supper that evening, and from the grim looks on their faces anybody would have guessed they were about to ride into battle.

That was sort of the way it was, Stark mused as he watched from the boardwalk in front of the hotel. The ranchers knew they were coming into town for a meeting with Juan Espina, a meeting that might determine the fates of all of them.

Earlier in the afternoon he had asked Sheriff Higgins to send deputies out to Antlers and the Boxed BT to summon the cattlemen to the town hall at eight o'clock. The sheriff agreed, adding that he might have some extra men on duty that night, in case of trouble.

Trouble seemed a distinct possibility. Enough men had witnessed Juan's drunken, angry performance earlier in the day in Chadwick's office and had spread the news around town. If the old man followed through on his stubborn threats, all hell was likely to break loose. Garrison was holding its breath tonight, even more so than before Stark had announced his verdict at the hearing the day before.

Matt Curry came up to Stark as Richmond, Tompkins, and their men rode by in the street. "They look like they're going off to war," Curry commented, unwittingly echoing the thought that had occurred to Stark.

"It *is* war," Stark said, "war for all the things they've built over the years. War between one way of life and an older way of life, for a change. Usually the struggle's between the old and the new, but not this time."

"You're talking about those Spanish land grants?"

Stark nodded. "I reckon that old Spanish king never knew how much trouble he was going to cause all these years later." He glanced at Curry. "I thought Billy Chadwick was going to have you help him keep an eye on Juan."

"Juan's all right now," Curry said. "Mr. Chadwick poured coffee down his throat all afternoon and got him sobered up. And Dolores read him the riot act pretty good, too." The young journalist grinned. "Juan promised he wouldn't get into any more mischief."

"Well, I hope not," Stark grunted. "Come on, we might as well get down to the town hall." He could see the riders dismounting and tying their horses in front of the building down the street.

"I'll be there in a minute," Curry said. "Excuse me, Judge."

Stark watched with a faint smile as Curry hurried

across the street to meet Don Alfonso Montoya and the young woman called Angelina, both of whom were obviously on their way to the town hall, too. Stark hadn't talked to the Mexican diplomat today, but he knew Montoya would stay here until everything was settled, so that he could give *El Presidente* Díaz a full report when he got back to Mexico City. Curry tugged his hat off when he stepped up on the boardwalk to greet the Montoyas, and Stark could see that the youngster was giving most of his attention to Angelina. Well, that wasn't surprising, Stark decided, considering that she was a mighty pretty girl.

The whole town knew about this meeting, of course, and a crowd was gathering outside the town hall. Stark had no intention of letting anyone in except the ranchers and their lawyer, Juan Espina, Billy Chadwick, and Don Alfonso Montoya. And Matt Curry, as the representative of the press, would have to attend, too.

Travis Richmond and Ben Tompkins were waiting outside the door of the town hall. Stark looked around at the men who had ridden into town with them but didn't see Richmond's son, Cord. Stark had been hoping that Richmond would leave his son home tonight; the situation was tense enough without that young firebrand around. Evidently Richmond had come to the same conclusion.

Neither were any of the smaller ranchers in attendance. As Stark came up to Richmond and Tompkins, he asked, "Are you two speaking for the other cattlemen in the valley tonight?"

Richmond nodded curtly. "We all agreed that would be best. Ben and I represent their interests as well as ours."

The Diablo Grant

"That's all right with me," Stark said. "Let's go on inside—but leave your men out here."

For a moment he thought they were going to argue with him, especially Tompkins. But then both ranchers issued low-voiced orders for their hands to remain outside, and they went in ahead of Stark. Matt Curry and the Montoyas were already inside, seated near the tables at the front of the room. Angelina had no real reason to be here, but Stark saw no point in offending her father by running her out. Besides, that would probably make Curry angry, too.

Richmond and Tompkins sat down on the other side of the aisle from Curry and the Montoyas. Stark paused beside them and asked, "Where's Fanning?"

"He'll be here," Tompkins said. "He durned well better be."

The lawyer from Santa Fe hurried in a few minutes later, after Stark had taken his place at the larger table. He nodded and said, "Good evening, Your Honor. I trust this meeting will be beneficial for all concerned."

"That's the general idea," Stark said dryly. "Sit down, Mr. Fanning. We're going to be pretty informal here tonight, and we'll get started as soon as Juan and Billy Chadwick show up."

Fanning nodded and sat down next to his clients, and they conferred in low voices for several minutes. Stark had laid his hat aside and opened his coat to get comfortable, but time still passed slowly. As the seconds ticked by, he began to worry. He took out a battered old watch from his vest pocket and flipped open the turnip. It was ten minutes past eight o'clock.

Chadwick knew good and well when this meeting

was supposed to begin. Hell, the whole town knew. Stark wondered what was keeping him and Juan.

He looked up as the door at the rear of the hall opened, expecting to see the two men entering. Chadwick was there, all right, but he was alone. Frowning, Stark called to him, "Where's your client, Counselor?"

Chadwick stopped in his tracks and looked around, an expression of confusion on his weathered face. "Isn't Juan here?" he asked.

A tingle of worry went through Stark. "No, he's not. I figured he'd be with you."

"I just went by the hotel and knocked on the door of his room. When there was no answer, I decided he had come on over here by himself."

Stark got to his feet. The other people in the room murmured in concern, but he cut through the noise by saying sharply, "I thought you were going to stay with him. Curry there said you'd been pouring coffee down him all afternoon."

"That's right," Chadwick said with a nod. "But Juan sobered up, and I thought it would be all right to go back to my office for a minute to pick up all the paperwork on this case. I told him to stay put until I got back, damn it!"

Stark took a deep breath. If Juan wasn't at the hotel—and he blamed sure wasn't here at the town hall—that meant he was out wandering around Garrison somewhere. And that was trouble waiting to happen. Big trouble.

"All right," Stark said. "No use worrying about what should have been done. Mr. Chadwick, Sheriff Higgins,

The Diablo Grant

I want you to come with me. The rest of you stay put. We'll be back as soon as we can." He reached for his hat.

"Where're we goin', Judge?" the sheriff asked.

"First thing we'll do is go back by the hotel, just to make sure Juan's not there somewhere. If he's not, we'll get your deputies, Sheriff, and we'll all split up and start looking. That old man's got to be *somewhere*."

Stark ignored the angry questions shouted to him by Tompkins and Richmond as he strode out of the town hall, trailed by the worried-looking Chadwick and Higgins. Stark figured he looked pretty anxious himself. This situation was already complicated enough; if anything happened to Juan it would bollix things up even more.

With Chadwick and Higgins behind him, Stark pushed through the crowd outside, paying no attention to their questions, either. The three men headed straight for the hotel, where Stark asked the startled desk clerk, "You seen Juan Espina coming or going lately?"

The young man shook his head. "No, sir, Your Honor. I haven't seen Señor Espina since this afternoon."

"He could've gone out the back way," Stark muttered to his companions. "Come on." He started climbing the stairs. Halfway up, he looked over his shoulder and asked Chadwick, "Did you check the girl's room? He could've been with her."

"There was no answer there, either," Chadwick replied.

Stark's frown deepened. He figured that maybe Juan and Dolores had left the hotel and were out in one of Garrison's cantinas, but he wanted to be sure they weren't upstairs before he launched a full-fledged search.

He had noticed downstairs that the key to Juan's room wasn't on its hook, and neither was Dolores's. That didn't necessarily mean anything, though; they could have taken the keys with them when they left. But as he hurried down the corridor toward the rooms, he recalled that Dolores had wanted to keep Juan from drinking and getting into trouble; it wasn't likely that she would go cantina-crawling with him now.

Stark reached the door of Juan's room and knocked loudly on it. "Juan!" he called. "You in there, Juan?"

There was no answer. Stark jerked his head at Chadwick, who went along the hall to the door of Dolores's room and rapped on it. "Dolores! It's Billy Chadwick. Are you in there?" After a moment he turned, looked at Stark with a shrug, and shook his head.

Warning bells were going off in Stark's brain. Something was badly wrong here, he sensed, and he needed to see what was inside the old Mexican's hotel room. He reached down and tried to twist the knob, only to find that the door was locked. He could send the sheriff downstairs to fetch a passkey from the desk, he knew, but that would mean waiting.

"Maybe you'd best look the other way, Sheriff," he growled to Higgins as he lifted his foot and drove his bootheel against the door, right beside the knob.

The door sprang open and crashed back against the wall. Stark went through the opening in a rush, palming out the LeMat as he did so. In a crouch he scanned the room, his keen eyes taking in everything that was revealed by the glow from a lamp on the bedside table.

The Diablo Grant

The lamp and the table on which it sat were about the only things undisturbed in the room. All the chairs had been turned over, as if in a struggle. The rug next to the bed was wadded up, probably kicked into an untidy heap by shuffling feet. The bedspread had been pulled partway off on the far side of the big four-poster. Stark looked past the foot of the bed and saw a pair of expensive, hand-tooled boots lying on the floor.

His blood turned to ice in his veins. He could tell that those boots had feet in them.

"What in blazes—" Chadwick exclaimed as he and Sheriff Higgins crowded into the room behind Stark.

"Looks like there was a big ruckus here," the lawman added.

"And one of the men who was fighting is still here," Stark said grimly as he circled the bed. He held the LeMat ready, but he saw quickly that he wasn't going to need it.

The man sprawled on the floor on the other side of the bed wasn't ever going to be a threat to anyone again.

From the looks of it, Juan Espina had pulled the bedspread off as he was struggling with his killer. It was draped across him, but it didn't cover his face. The bulging eyes, the protruding tongue, and the scrawny neck with its ugly blue bruises were all quite visible. The grisly sight drew a heartfelt curse from Stark.

Sheriff Higgins let out a low whistle. "Somebody's done choked the life right out of that old man!"

Stark holstered his gun and knelt beside the body. He placed a couple of fingers on Juan's neck, checking for a pulse. He wasn't surprised when he found none. Juan's eyes were already completely glazed over.

He had been dead for several minutes, maybe as long as half an hour.

"When did you leave him here?" Stark asked Chadwick.

"About forty-five minutes ago, I reckon," the lawyer replied, his voice tight with anger and shock. "Long enough to go to my office, pick up those papers, and then come back by here. Then I went on to the town hall when I didn't get any answer to my knock." Chadwick paused. "I was afraid then that something was wrong, but I was hoping Juan had gone on to the meeting by himself."

"Somebody must've showed up here right after you left the first time," Stark mused, still on one knee beside the corpse. "Juan was likely already dead when you knocked on the door."

"It looks like he put up quite a fight," Chadwick said. "Maybe somebody else on this floor heard something."

Stark considered the suggestion, then shrugged. "We'll check with the other guests, of course, but there's nobody else in the rooms close by. The ones that are occupied are down at the other end of the hall. I knew that when I told the clerk to put Juan and Dolores in these rooms close to mine."

"Speakin' of that girl," Higgins said, "I reckon we'd better find her right quick. If she happened to see who done this to ol' Juan, then the killer'd likely want to get rid of her, too."

"Then why didn't he just go ahead and strangle her, like he did Juan?" Chadwick asked.

Stark stood up. "Could be she ran out before the killer could get hold of her. But then it stands to reason she would've screamed her head off for help."

The Diablo Grant

With a worried look on his long face, Higgins asked, "You don't reckon that little gal could've done this, do you, Judge?"

Stark glanced at the body of Juan Espina, who looked even more frail and fragile now than he had in life. "I reckon she could have," Stark said. "It wouldn't have taken anybody real strong to choke that old man to death. But I can't see that she would have a reason to do something like that. The way I understand it, she and Juan have always been friends."

Higgins rubbed his stubbled jaw. "Still, I better get my men started lookin' for her right away."

He had just turned toward the doorway when a scream ripped through the room. Stark's head jerked around, and he saw Dolores standing there in the open doorway, her hands pressed to her mouth. She shrieked again past her wide-spread fingers.

"Grab her!" Stark grunted to Billy Chadwick, who was the closest one to the young woman.

Chadwick stepped over and took hold of her arm, but Dolores wasn't going anywhere anyway. Her gaze was fixed on the fancy boots sticking out beyond the foot of the bed, and Stark figured she recognized them as one of Juan's recent purchases. She took a deep, ragged breath and asked, "Is it . . . is it Juan?"

Chadwick said, "I'm afraid so, Dolores."

"He is hurt?" she asked, her voice trembling. "He is . . ." She was unable to complete the question.

Stark answered it anyway, deciding not to soften the blow so that he could see how Dolores was going to react. He said, "Juan's dead, Dolores. Somebody choked him to death."

She let out a wail and might have collapsed if

119

Chadwick hadn't grabbed her other arm. "This cannot be," she moaned. "He cannot be dead!"

Stark stepped over to her, and his voice was a little gentler—but not much—as he asked, "Where have you been for the past hour, Dolores?"

"I was being fitted for a dress . . . at Señora Murray's shop. Juan made the arrangements earlier today, and I was to come back this evening for the measurements— Ohhhh!" Another wave of sobbing overwhelmed her. She managed to pull a lace handkerchief from the stylish little reticule she was carrying and crumpled it against her eyes.

Stark exchanged a look with Chadwick and Sheriff Higgins. He said, "This Mrs. Murray the girl mentioned—you know her?"

Chadwick nodded. "One of the most respectable women in town, Judge. If Dolores has been down at her shop for the past hour, that makes it pretty clear she didn't have anything to do with this."

Dolores gasped and wailed again, as if horrified that anyone could have even suspected her of Juan's murder. Stark figured he couldn't blame her for feeling that way. From all indications she was very fond of the old man, and she didn't have the naturally suspicious nature that a man in Stark's line of work developed.

"All right, you'd best get her out of here, Counselor. Take her back to her own room and then see if the hotel has a maid or a cook or somebody who can stay with her for a while. Sheriff, you can send for the undertaker, then get back up here and stay beside the body until someone comes for it."

Higgins nodded. "What'll you be doin', Your Honor?"

"I'm going to start asking questions," Stark said as he glanced one last time at the contorted, frozen features of Juan Espina. "And, by God, I'd better get some answers."

Chapter Nine

Stark clattered down the stairs to the lobby and found the clerk standing behind the desk, anxiously shifting his weight from foot to foot.

"I heard screams up there," the young man said. "Is something wrong, Judge?"

"You could say that," grunted Stark. "That gal called Dolores just went up there a few minutes ago, right?"

The clerk bobbed his head. "That's right, Your Honor. She left the hotel over an hour ago, and she just got back."

That information corroborated Dolores's story. Stark nodded and said, "Did you see anybody else come and go during the past hour?"

"Through the lobby, you mean?"

Stark suppressed his impatience and said, "That's right, through the lobby. Or anywhere else around the hotel, for that matter."

"Well, I'm supposed to stay on duty here at the desk, so all I could see would be the lobby."

Stark fought the urge to take hold of the fellow's neck and shake some straight answers out of him.

"A couple of men left about half an hour ago," the clerk continued. "They're whiskey drummers, and I think they were on their way to call on some of the saloon owners."

"Know these gents well, do you?"

"They've been staying here for several years now, every time their work brings them through this part of the territory."

Stark nodded slowly. A couple of drummers, especially ones who were well-known in Garrison, didn't sound like likely suspects. He couldn't rule out anybody, though. He got the names of the two men from the clerk, then said, "Nobody else came or went during that time?"

"Well, not through the lobby. And I'm supposed to stay here at the desk—"

"I know," Stark cut in. Taking note of the clerk's nervousness, he said pointedly, "But you didn't stay here in the lobby all the time, did you?"

At that blunt accusation the clerk opened and closed his mouth several times, then crumpled rapidly under Stark's stern glare.

"I just went out back to the, ah, facilities for a minute," he said. "I wasn't gone from the desk for more than five minutes, I swear."

"So somebody could've gotten past you," Stark said heavily.

"Well, it's not that so much—"

Stark seized on the indecisiveness in the clerk's

voice. "You saw somebody else back there, didn't you?"

The clerk glanced around, looking like a wild animal that wanted to bolt. "I really shouldn't say anything. I don't even know what's wrong—"

"Juan Espina is dead," Stark said. "He was murdered."

"Oh, Lord," the clerk breathed. "That old Mexican who . . . who was going to take over Diablo Valley? But that means—"

"Means what?" Stark pushed.

The clerk let out a moan. He was sweating now. "We went to school together," he said.

"You and Espina?" Stark asked, confused now.

"No, me and Cord. He never liked me. He used to beat me up. Oh, hell, he's going to kill me. . . ."

"Cord Richmond?" Stark felt his pulse pound.

The clerk nodded shakily.

"You saw Cord Richmond here at the hotel tonight?"

"He . . . he was coming out the rear door of the hotel just as I was about to leave the outhouse. I stayed back where he couldn't see me." The clerk's voice took on a bitter edge. "We have facilities here inside the hotel, of course, but the employees aren't allowed to use them. They're for guests only. We have to use the old two-holer out back."

At the moment Stark didn't give a damn about the clerk's grievances. He said, "Let me make sure I've got this straight. You saw Cord Richmond sneaking out of the hotel earlier tonight?"

"About forty-five, maybe fifty minutes ago. Less than an hour, I know that."

Stark cursed under his breath. He wasn't surprised

to hear that Cord had been here in town tonight. Travis Richmond had left the young hothead at their ranch, but Cord hadn't been able to stay away.

Or maybe Richmond had *sent* his son here, to sneak in the back door of the hotel and creep upstairs and dispose of the old man who represented such a threat to the way of life they had built in Diablo Valley.

"You're sure it was Cord Richmond?"

"It was him, all right," the clerk declared as he used a handkerchief to mop sweat off his forehead. "Like I said, we went to school together here in Garrison. I'm not likely to forget somebody who pulled down my pants in front of all the girls."

"No, I reckon that'd stay with you, all right," Stark said. "You got anything else you need to tell me?"

The clerk shook his head.

"Thanks," Stark told him. "You sit tight, and don't let anybody else upstairs until the sheriff tells you it's all right."

"Sure, Your Honor."

Stark left the hotel and headed for the town hall. The men waiting there would be getting a mite restless by now, and Stark couldn't blame them. Their fates were bound up in what happened tonight—maybe in more ways than one.

He was pelted with questions as soon as he shoved the door open and strode into the meeting room. He ignored them, walked up to face Travis Richmond, and asked a question of his own. "Where's your son tonight?"

Richmond glared at him in a mixture of anger and confusion. "I left him out at Antlers. Figured it would be better that way. Cord loses his temper mighty easy."

"I remember," Stark said. "I remember him threatening to kill Juan Espina."

"He was just blowing off steam," Richmond said with a curt gesture. "Cord wouldn't hurt anybody."

"Somebody did. Somebody just strangled the old man. He's dead."

"What!" Matt Curry cried, bounding to his feet. Beside him, Angelina Montoya let out a soft cry and brought a hand to her mouth. Her father tightened his arm around her shoulders.

"This is unbelievable!" Don Alfonso exclaimed. "How could such a thing happen?"

"That's what I intend to find out," Stark said. Richmond was on his feet now, glaring at him. Stark met the rancher's angry gaze squarely and went on, "Your son was seen sneaking out of the hotel tonight, just about the time Juan was killed."

"That's impossible!" Richmond snorted. "Cord's hotheaded sometimes, I'll admit that's true. But he wouldn't kill anyone, especially an old man like that!"

"Then you won't mind if we ride out to your ranch and question him."

Richmond hesitated, and Stark saw the faintest flicker of doubt in the man's eyes. Perhaps deep down, Richmond wasn't completely convinced that his son was innocent of Juan's murder.

But he said stubbornly, "That's fine. We'll go out there and you'll see how ridiculous this accusation is. And I warn you, Judge Stark, I intend to file a complaint with your superiors about this high-handed treatment!"

"I'll be glad to handle that for you, Travis," Alfred Fanning said smoothly.

The Diablo Grant

Stark ignored the lawyer and said to Ben Tompkins, "What about you? You got anything to say?"

The burly cattleman shrugged. "Travis and me have had our differences in the past, but I don't think that boy of his would kill anybody—although he does fly off the handle pretty bad sometimes."

Richmond shot Tompkins a sharp glance, as if saying he wasn't helping matters with answers like that, but Tompkins didn't seem to notice. Stark jerked his head toward the doorway and said, "Let's go. I'll stop by the livery stable and pick up my Appaloosa."

"I'm going, too," Matt Curry said, and no one argued with him as they filed out of the town hall.

The punchers from Antlers and the Boxed BT wanted to know what was going on, of course, but Stark warned everyone who had been inside the meeting room to keep their mouths shut about the matter. He ran into Billy Chadwick and Sheriff Boone Higgins on his way to the livery stable and quickly filled them in on what he had learned from the desk clerk at the hotel.

"Cord Richmond has been in plenty of scrapes before, but nothing this bad," Chadwick commented. "The sheriff and I had better ride out to Antlers with you, Judge."

"I figured the two of you would come along. Everything squared away at the hotel?"

"That gal Dolores is in her room with one of the maids," Higgins said, "and I got a deputy posted right outside the door to keep an eye on 'em—for Dolores's protection as much as anything, I reckon. And the undertaker's got the old man's body down to his place. He's the county coroner, too, so everything's bein' handled legal-like."

Stark nodded in satisfaction. "Let's fetch our horses and get moving. I don't want Richmond getting any ideas about riding on ahead and warning his son."

Evidently that hadn't occurred to Richmond, because he and his men were mounted up and waiting in front of the town hall, along with Tompkins and the Boxed BT riders, when Stark, Chadwick, and Higgins joined them a few minutes later. It was possible, of course, that Richmond had sent a rider on ahead, but Stark hoped the man's determination to prove the accusations against his son false would have prevented such a maneuver.

The large group of riders pounded out of Garrison, heading toward Diablo Valley and the Antlers ranch. Richmond rode stiffly, staring straight ahead. Stark glanced over at the man in the moonlight and saw the mixture of anger, pride, and fear on his face. Once again Stark felt a twinge of regret at his part in the trouble that had led to this nighttime ride. But the law was the law, he reminded himself again, and he was sworn to uphold it.

It took over an hour to reach the headquarters of Richmond's spread. As the riders approached, Stark saw lights burning in the big ranch house. Apparently Cord Richmond was still up.

He must have heard them coming, because he stepped out onto the veranda as the riders came into the yard. He called out, "Dad? Is that you?"

"That's right, Cord," Richmond said as he reined in.

Enough light from the house spilled through the open doorway behind Cord for the young man to see that his father was accompanied by Ben Tompkins, Stark,

The Diablo Grant

Chadwick, Sheriff Higgins, and Matt Curry. The punchers from Antlers and the Boxed BT hung back a little. Cord frowned and asked, "What's going on here? What happened at that meeting in town?"

"There wasn't any meeting," Richmond said.

Stark rested his hands on the saddlehorn and leaned forward. "I reckon you knew that already, didn't you, Cord?"

Cord narrowed his eyes. "What the hell do you mean by that? What are you doing out here anyway, Judge?"

"We came to ask you some questions." Stark's gaze touched on the holstered six-gun on Cord's hip. Had the youngster been expecting trouble? Otherwise, why would he be armed, here in his own house?

"Questions about what?" Cord asked harshly. "I don't have to answer any damn questions!"

Billy Chadwick said, "I'd advise you to cooperate, Cord. You don't want to make things worse."

Cord looked at his father. "What's going on here, Dad?"

Richmond asked heavily, "Were you in town tonight, Cord?"

"You told me to stay here—"

"I know what I told you. Did you ride into Garrison anyway?"

For a second, Cord didn't answer. Then he sneered and said, "What business is it of anybody's if I did?"

"You were seen sneaking out of the hotel," Stark said flatly. "And that was right before the meeting between Juan Espina and your pa and Tompkins was supposed to take place."

"Damn it!" Cord ripped out as his hand flashed toward the gun on his hip. "You won't railroad me for killing that old bastard!"

"Cord!" his father cried, but he was too late. Cord already had the revolver out and was lifting it.

Beside Stark, Sheriff Higgins was clawing at his own gun. But Stark knew he wasn't going to get it out in time to prevent Cord from getting off a shot. Chadwick was also drawing his gun, his motion smoother and more efficient than the sheriff's but still not fast enough.

Stark didn't want any shooting. If guns started banging, the cowboys ranged behind them might jump into the fracas, too, drawing and firing out of instinct. Then innocent folks would get killed, and an already bad situation would get a lot messier. Stark jabbed his bootheels into the Appaloosa's flanks, and the big horse lunged forward. Stark left the saddle in a diving tackle, leaping over the railing along the edge of the porch and crashing into Cord Richmond. He slapped the young man's gun hand aside with his left hand as he drove his right fist into Cord's jaw.

Cord was big and husky, and the fight didn't go out of him easily. As his father yelled, "Stop it!" and Tompkins shouted, "Hold your fire!" to the Boxed BT men, Cord shrugged off Stark's punch and slashed at the judge's head with the barrel of the revolver. Stark ducked under the blow and let the gun knock his hat off, then hooked a hard left into Cord's midsection. The impact staggered Cord, knocking him back a step and setting him up for the right uppercut that Stark launched next. Stark's fist crashed into Cord's jaw a second time, and this one did the job. Cord was thrown back against the wall of the house, and the gun slipped out of his fingers and thumped to the planks of the porch. He folded up, went to his knees, and slumped forward.

"Just sit there nice and easy," Sheriff Higgins warned behind Stark, and the judge cast a glance over his shoulder to see both Higgins and Chadwick covering Travis Richmond and Ben Tompkins. Matt Curry was sitting his horse off to one side, his eyes wide as he watched the confrontation.

Stark was breathing heavily from his brief fight with Cord, but at least nobody had been killed so far. He bent over and scooped up his hat, punching it back into shape before settling it on his head. "You heard your boy," he said to Richmond. "He said nobody was going to railroad him for killing Juan—before any of us even mentioned Juan was dead. That sounds like guilty knowledge to me, Richmond."

The cattleman's leathery face was pulled into a gaunt mask. Clearly the same thought had occurred to him.

Stark went on, "You didn't send anybody out here ahead of us to warn him, did you?"

Richmond shook his head jerkily. "No. No, Cord shouldn't have known the old man was dead. Not unless he was really there." He seized on a faint hope. "But just because he was in the hotel, that doesn't mean he killed Espina!"

Stark shrugged. "You're right, it doesn't. But it gives us plenty of cause to take him back to town, put him in a jail cell, and wait until he's ready to answer a few questions. Doesn't it, Sheriff?"

"Afraid so, Mr. Richmond," Higgins said. "We got to take Cord in, sir."

Stark glanced around the yard. Tompkins would

probably side with Richmond if it came down to that, and the representatives of the law were definitely outnumbered here. They couldn't take Cord Richmond into custody unless his father cooperated.

Richmond drew a deep breath and let it out in a heavy sigh. His shoulders slumped. "I know. Do what you have to do, Sheriff."

It was a bitter defeat, Stark thought, probably the worst the old cattleman had ever endured. But he sat silently on his horse, head down, while Stark and Higgins brought Cord Richmond around, handcuffed him, and got him on a horse.

As Stark was swinging up into his own saddle again, he caught Matt Curry's eye and said, "This story for your paper just keeps getting better and better, doesn't it?"

"Not anymore," Curry said hollowly. "I never figured all these things would happen. I had no idea . . ."

Stark nodded and pulled the Appaloosa around, heading the animal toward town. Maybe there was a human being inside that journalist after all, he thought.

"I didn't kill the old man," Cord said stubbornly from inside his jail cell. He was sitting on the narrow bunk, his elbows on his knees and his hands clasped together in front of him. It was a posture of despair, but his head was still up, and he was glaring defiantly at Stark and Higgins, who stood outside the cell. "I was in town, all right. I went to the hotel; I'm not going to lie about that. But I didn't kill anybody."

"Why were you there?" Stark asked.

Cord took a deep breath. "I figured I'd try one more time to scare that old bastard into giving up his claim to the valley. I thought maybe I could scare him so bad he'd never show his face around here again."

"But when he argued with you, you choked the life out of him instead."

Cord shook his head vehemently. "No, damn it, I didn't! I never got the chance to argue with him. He was dead when I got there!"

Stark frowned. He hadn't expected Cord to take this tack. "How'd you get into the room?" he asked. "It was locked when Chadwick and the sheriff and I got there. I kicked it open."

"Well, it wasn't locked when *I* got there. Espina didn't come to the door when I knocked, so I tried the knob. The door opened, and I went in." Cord stood up and paced back and forth in the narrow cell. "He was lying there on the floor by the bed."

"And he was already dead?" Higgins asked.

"Yeah. Yeah, he was." Cord's lips pulled back from his teeth in a grimace. "I got to tell you, Sheriff, for a minute there I was glad the son of a bitch was dead. But then I realized how it would look if anybody found him while I was around like that." He laughed humorlessly. "I figured folks would jump to the wrong conclusion—and just look where I am now!" He spread his hands to indicate his surroundings.

"What did you do after you discovered Juan's body?" Stark asked.

"I looked around for the key to the room. It was on the dresser. I left and locked the door after me, then threw the key away in the alley out behind the hotel. I figured the longer it was before anybody else found him, the better off I'd be. I wanted to get well away from town before that happened. I didn't think anybody saw me as I was leaving." Again he gave a bleak chuckle. "Reckon I was wrong."

"All right," Stark said with a curt nod. "You sure that's all you've got to say?"

"It's the truth," Cord snapped. "What else do you want?"

Stark didn't answer. Instead he inclined his head toward the door leading from the cellblock into the sheriff's office, and Higgins followed him out.

When the cellblock door was shut and locked, Higgins rubbed his jaw and asked Stark, "You believe him, Judge?"

"Well, it *could* have happened that way, I reckon," Stark said slowly. "But it sure doesn't seem likely. Cord's story is mighty weak, and there's still the fact that he pulled his gun and tried to shoot his way out when we confronted him earlier tonight at Antlers." He shook his head decisively. "Nope, the way things stand now, I just don't believe him. I think he lost his head and killed Juan Espina, and he's come up with that yarn about Juan already being dead just to try to talk his way out of trouble."

"Got to admit, that's the way it looks to me, too," the sheriff said. "Lordy, this business sure has turned into a mess, ain't it?"

"That's the truth," Stark agreed.

"What are you goin' to do now, Judge?"

Stark shook his head. "I don't know. With Juan dead, the land grant issue is moot. And murder's a state crime, not a federal one, so I have no jurisdiction over that part of the case. Reckon I ought to wire Washington and see where I'm needed next, since my job here is over."

The Diablo Grant

Higgins looked alarmed. "You ain't goin' to do that, are you? I could sure use a hand sortin' all this out, Judge, if you could see your way clear to stayin' around for a few days."

Stark slapped the lawman on the shoulder. "Don't worry, Sheriff. I don't like walking away from the table until the hand is over." He glanced at the cellblock door, thinking about the prisoner on the other side. "And I've got a hunch there are a few more cards waiting to be dealt."

Chapter Ten

At Stark's suggestion, Sheriff Higgins swore in several special deputies. It seemed unlikely to Stark that Travis Richmond would try to break his son out of jail—Richmond could have prevented Cord's being jailed in the first place, if he had been willing to go against the law—but it was hard to predict what a father might do to help his son. There would be guards on duty at the jail twenty-four hours a day until all this was settled.

Once that chore was taken care of, there was nothing else for Stark to do, so he went back to the hotel and tried to get some sleep. It wasn't easy. He kept seeing the dead, twisted features of Juan Espina, and somehow the old man seemed to be accusing him of something. Stark knew it wasn't his fault Juan was dead—but that didn't make sleep come any more easily.

When he went to the sheriff's office the next morning, he was still tired, with a weary ache in his shoulders and a gritty feeling behind his eyelids. Boone Higgins was sitting behind the desk, looking equally worn out.

"Cord still singing the same tune?" Stark asked as he picked up a ladder-back chair, reversed it, and straddled it. Since, as far as he knew, he wasn't going to be conducting any legal business in the near future, he had packed away the black suit and was dressed today in the denim pants, bib-front shirt, and black vest he had been wearing when he first arrived in Garrison.

"He ain't changed his story a bit," the sheriff replied. "Still says ol' Juan was dead when he found him. I *have* turned up one more piece of evidence, though."

Stark's interest perked up, and he forgot his exhaustion for a moment. "What's that?"

"Took a look around that alley behind the hotel a little while ago." Higgins took something from his shirt pocket and tossed it onto the desk. "Found that back there, next to a rain barrel."

Stark picked up the object. "The key to Juan's room?"

"Yep. I went inside the hotel and tried it. Opened that door right up."

"Well, just because the key was where Cord said he threw it away, that doesn't mean he's innocent. He admitted he wanted as much time to get away as possible before the body was found."

"Yeah, I reckon you're right. If I was him and I'd killed the old man, I'd've locked the door on the way out, too, providin' I could keep a cool head long enough to do that."

Stark cuffed his Stetson to the back of his head and frowned. "It would take some pretty clear thinking," he admitted. "And most folks who had just gotten through choking an old man to death might not be that level-headed."

Higgins shrugged. "Way I see it, this key ain't proof one way or t'other."

"You're right," Stark told him. "Maybe I'll have another talk with Cord." Not that it was likely to do any good, he thought.

Before he could get up and go into the cellblock, however, the door of the sheriff's office opened again, and Billy Chadwick strode into the room. "Morning, Judge," he said. "I was hoping I might find you here. Howdy, Boone."

Chadwick looked worried about something. Stark asked, "Something else hasn't happened, has it?"

"Well, as a matter of fact, it has," Chadwick said. He reached into his pocket and took out an envelope. "Juan gave this to me a couple of days ago—before your final ruling in the land grant case, in fact—and told me not to open it unless something happened to him. In all the confusion, I almost forgot about it, but I got it out of my office safe this morning and opened it up." He slid a folded piece of paper from the envelope and held it out toward Stark. "See for yourself, Your Honor."

Stark hesitated. This case sure as hell didn't need any more twists and turns. But ignorance wouldn't help now, so he took the paper, spread it out on his knee, and read the words written there in Juan's familiar, spidery hand.

"This is a will," he said in surprise a moment later.

"It's written in Spanish, but I can tell it's a last will and testament."

"It certainly is. I don't know about you, Judge, but I guess I assumed last night that Juan died without any heirs." Chadwick gestured at the document. "As you can see, that's not the case."

"What in blazes are you talkin' about?" Sheriff Higgins asked. "You mean ol' Juan left his holdin's to somebody else?"

"At the time that will was written," Chadwick explained, "Juan couldn't have known he would have any estate to leave to anyone, because the land grant claim hadn't been settled yet. But he perhaps had more sense than any of us really gave him credit for, because he prepared for the future as if he knew he was going to win the case."

"Well, what's it say?" Higgins burst out. "Who'd he leave everything to?"

"The logical person," Stark said quietly. "The only person he seemed to really care about. Dolores."

Higgins sank back in his chair and stared. "Juan left the whole Diablo Valley to a *whore*?"

Stark ignored the question from the thunderstruck lawman and looked at Chadwick. "Are you sure this is Juan's handwriting?"

"It matches every sample I've seen," Chadwick said.

"Yeah, I thought so, too," Stark admitted. "These days, most folks have a lawyer draw up their wills, but there's nothing illegal about doing it this way. You know what this means, Billy."

Chadwick nodded. "I'm afraid I do."

"Wait just a minute," Higgins protested. "How could he leave her the Diablo Valley when he didn't even know when he wrote that will if he owned it or not?"

"He didn't have to know," Stark said. "This document is worded so that anything Juan owned at the time of his death goes to Dolores. That would include Diablo Valley."

"Lordy mercy! People ain't goin' to like this."

"I reckon you're right about that," Stark told the sheriff. "But there's not much they can do about it. Thanks to my ruling in the hearing, Juan was the legal owner of Diablo Valley at the time of his death. That means Dolores inherits the valley, along with the rest of Juan's estate."

"Which won't amount to much," Chadwick pointed out. "This makes me think, Judge—"

"Yeah, me, too," Stark cut in. "It's a good thing Dolores has such a good alibi for last evening, because that will is one hell of a motive for murder."

The sheriff said, "Wait just a darn minute. We got Cord Richmond locked up for killin' the old man. Now you're sayin' you two think that gal might've done it?"

Stark shook his head. "Not under these circumstances. But if things had been just a little bit different, well, Dolores would've been a ready-made suspect."

"I guess I'd better go over to the hotel and break the news to her," Chadwick said. "Want to come along, Judge?"

Stark stood up. "Don't mind if I do."

They crossed the street to the hotel and went upstairs, where they found one of Higgins's deputies standing in front of the door to Dolores's room, a rifle in the crook of his arm. The man, recognizing both of them, nodded a greeting and stepped aside. Chadwick

The Diablo Grant

knocked on the door, and a weary voice answered from inside, *"Sí? Quién es?"*

"Billy Chadwick," the lawyer replied. "And Judge Stark is with me, too."

A second later a key rattled in the lock and the door swung open. Dolores stood there in a dressing gown, her face still red and swollen from crying. *"Buenos dias,"* she said. "Do you need to speak with me, Señor Chadwick?"

Chadwick took off his hat, and Stark followed his example. "Yes, there is something I need to talk to you about, Dolores," Chadwick said. "Could we come in?"

"Sí. I am sorry." She stepped back.

"No need to be sorry," Chadwick told her. Stark shut the door behind them, and the lawyer went on, "There's been another . . . development . . . in Juan's death."

"I know that Señor Cord Richmond is in jail," Dolores said. "He is the one who killed Juan, no?"

"It certainly looks like he's the one," Chadwick said. "But that's not why we're here. Can you read, Dolores?" He took the envelope from his coat pocket.

Looking slightly embarrassed, she shook her head.

"Well, this paper says that Juan wanted you to have everything he owned when he died. It's a will, Dolores, and he left his entire estate to you. You now own Diablo Valley."

She stared at him, her eyes gradually widening until it seemed they would pop out of her head. Stark figured that most women in Dolores's line of work had a bit of actress in them, but he didn't believe this young woman was skillful enough to be faking the emotions she displayed now. She appeared to be utterly stunned by Chadwick's revelation.

"This . . . this thing is not possible," she said after a moment. "I do not believe it."

"I've looked it over myself," Chadwick said, "and so has Judge Stark, and we're convinced it's not only genuine, but legal and binding. Isn't that right, Judge?"

"Billy's telling you the truth, Dolores," Stark said with a nod. "The valley's yours."

"But . . . but why?" She looked at them in confusion. "Juan was my friend, but we never even . . . we never . . . he would not let me—"

"That's all right," Chadwick said gently. "We understand. But you said it yourself, Dolores. You and Juan were friends. Such good friends that I reckon he wanted to be sure you were taken care of after he was gone."

Abruptly Dolores buried her face in her hands, her shoulders shaking as she sobbed. Stark and Chadwick looked at each other uncomfortably. Neither had had a lot of experience with crying women—nor wanted any more now.

"We'll leave you alone now," Chadwick told her. "You'd better come over to my office later, when you're feeling a little better. We'll have to file this will with the court, but it's just a matter of routine. You tell the deputy outside when you're ready to come see me, and he can bring you over to the office."

She nodded her head. "*Sí*. I will come."

Chadwick patted her awkwardly on the shoulder. "You just take it easy now. I know everything's been hard to understand lately, but we'll get it all sorted out."

Dolores nodded again, and Stark and Chadwick left as gracefully as they could. When they were back on

The Diablo Grant

the boardwalk outside the hotel, Chadwick blew out a breath and said, "I've seen Mexican cattle brands that weren't as jumbled up as all this."

Stark nodded in agreement. "I reckon it beats any skillet of snakes I'ever saw, too. But there's one thing that's pretty certain."

"What's that?" Chadwick asked.

"Folks around here weren't very happy when an old drunk wound up with Diablo Valley in his pocket. How are they going to feel now that the whole thing is owned by a Mexican whore?"

Chadwick looked at him grimly but didn't say anything. He didn't have to.

Both of them already knew the answer to that question.

When Matt Curry glanced up from his desk and saw a woman in a shawl passing by on the boardwalk outside the newspaper office, for a second he thought it was Angelina Montoya. His heart jumped in anticipation of seeing the young woman again.

But the visitor wasn't Angelina, he saw as she turned and came through the door into the office. Her figure was much too lush, and when she lowered the shawl around her shoulders, he saw the coarser but still attractive features of Dolores.

"Hello," Matt said as he came to his feet. "What can I do for you, Dolores?"

"I . . . I need your advice, Señor Curry," she said hesitantly. "You were so helpful to Juan, and now I do not know what to do."

"Well, I don't know how much help I was to Juan, the way things turned out—"

"He was very grateful to you, Señor Curry. I know this."

"Why don't you sit down?" Matt gestured to the chair in front of his desk. "I'll be glad to do whatever I can for you, Dolores, especially under the circumstances. Do you need someone to help you arrange Juan's funeral?"

"No, I have already spoken to the priest at the church. That will be taken care of. This . . . this is something else." She took a deep breath, and Matt could see how shaken she was.

"Don't worry," he told her gently. "Whatever it is, we'll figure out a way to handle it."

"I hope so. I do not know what to do with all that land."

Matt frowned. "What land?"

"Diablo Valley. Juan gave it to me. Señor Chadwick has what he called a . . . a will."

Matt's eyes widened, and his pulse began to pound in his head. "Juan left a will?" he asked in amazement.

Dolores nodded her head shyly. "*Sí*. Señor Chadwick says everything Juan owned when he died is now mine." She let out a little moan. "I do not know what to do!"

As he leaned back in his chair, thunderstruck, Matt thought about what this new development would mean. It had been sensational enough when Juan's claim to Diablo Valley had been upheld by Judge Stark. Now, with Dolores claiming the valley by right of inheritance, the story had just become even more of an attention-grabber. It would get play in newspapers from coast to coast—

Matt caught himself. He had begun to think that

The Diablo Grant

maybe his actions of the past couple of weeks had been less than admirable, considering his motives, and now here he was doing it again, thinking in terms of how much exposure he could give the story in the *Observer* rather than how it would affect the people involved. Maybe Judge Stark was right about him; maybe there wasn't a heart inside him at all, just a printing press.

Thinking about the burly, bearded jurist prompted Matt to ask, "Has Judge Stark seen this will of Juan's?"

Dolores nodded. "*Sí.* He and Señor Chadwick brought it to my room at the hotel. He said it was real and that I own Diablo Valley now that Juan is dead."

Another thought occurred to Matt, and he frowned again as he asked, "They don't think you had anything to do with Juan's murder, do they?"

"*Madre de Dios!* No, Señor Curry. They know I could never, never hurt Juan!"

Matt felt a little ashamed of himself. He said emphatically, "That's what I think, too. I know that you were Juan's best friend. Even if you didn't have an alibi, I'd know you were innocent."

Dolores shook her head. "I do not understand this word alibi, but I know I did not hurt Juan." She leaned forward and asked pitifully, "What do I do now, Señor Curry? I do not want Diablo Valley!"

"Well, I don't see that you've got much choice in the matter. The valley belonged to Juan, and now it belongs to you, at least legally. Do you know about the arrangement Judge Stark planned to set up between Juan and the ranchers out there?"

"The arrangement Juan said he would not accept?"

"That's right," Matt said. "It's really quite fair, Dolores, and it would give you plenty of money to live on without ruining Travis Richmond and Ben Tompkins and the other cattlemen. Do you think you could accept it, even though Juan didn't like the idea?"

"I do not know," she said slowly.

"I really think it's the best solution." Matt stood up, came out from behind the desk, and put a hand on her shoulder. "You think it over," he told her. "And remember, anything I can do to help you, I will."

"*Sí.*" She summoned up a smile. "*Muchas gracias,* Señor Curry. I do not know what I would do if it was not for you."

Matt smiled down at her. "Don't worry about that. I'm just glad I can help."

Suddenly Matt sensed something, and he looked up to see Angelina Montoya watching him through the front window, her dark eyes fixed on him with a peculiar intensity. He realized he was standing there grinning at Dolores, his hand on her shoulder, as she smiled up tremulously at him. He took his hand away quickly, but Dolores didn't seem to notice the abruptness of the gesture.

"You can go on back to the hotel now," he told her. "I'll talk this over with Judge Stark and Mr. Chadwick. I'm sure it can all be worked out, Dolores."

"Thank you again," she said softly as she rose to her feet.

Angelina was still standing outside watching, and Matt hoped like blazes that Dolores didn't do something rash like hug or kiss him in gratitude. He had been spending every spare minute with Angelina, at least all the minutes she could steal away from her father, and he knew that she possessed a jealous streak.

That was evident when Dolores left the newspaper

The Diablo Grant

office a moment later and Angelina entered as if she had just arrived. The two young women passed each other on the boardwalk outside the doorway, and although Dolores smiled, Angelina merely regarded her with a cool, haughty stare. Dolores hurried on, and Angelina came on into the office.

Matt felt the force of that stare as he smiled and said, "Good morning, señorita. I hope you slept well."

"I slept very well," Angelina replied. "What did that . . . person want?"

"Dolores just needed a little advice," Matt said. "She came to me because I had befriended her and Juan when all this started."

"And what is her problem?" Angelina asked, a trace of imperiousness in her voice.

"Well, Juan left a will when he died. Dolores has inherited all of his holdings—which means the Diablo Valley."

The cool mask dropped from Angelina's features. "My father must know about this," she said breathlessly. "The Mexican government will wish for Señor Espina's last wishes to be upheld."

Matt nodded. "I know. And I reckon they will be. According to Dolores, Judge Stark has already seen the will, and he said it looks like the real thing to him. I was on my way to hunt up the judge and Billy Chadwick and talk to them about all this."

"I will come with you," Angelina said without hesitation. "And then I will go back to the hotel and tell my father what I have learned."

Matt reached for his hat and coat, pleased that news of this unexpected development had made Angelina forget her brief attack of jealousy. "I'll be glad to have you with me," he told her as he shrugged into his coat. He put his hat on, then linked arms with her and led her out of the office. The warmth of her arm felt good against his.

"This is a very strange business," Angelina mused as they started down the boardwalk. "Just when you think it is over—"

"Something else happens," Matt finished for her.

That was sure enough true. And with everything that had gone before, Matt had to wonder what was going to happen *next*.

Chapter Eleven

Stark strolled with Billy Chadwick to the local bank, where the lawyer needed to take care of some business for one of his other clients. Both men nodded to Edmund Wells as they stood at a teller's window and Chadwick deposited some funds. The banker was talking to his head teller and gave them only a curt nod in return. Wells didn't look happy these days, and Stark decided it would be best not to mention the latest twist that the case of the Espina land grant had taken. Like almost everyone else in Garrison, Wells was already upset enough about Stark's decision to uphold the grant. There was no need to make things worse.

Chadwick seemed to feel the same way. He didn't say anything about the will Juan had left, but as the teller was completing the paperwork for his transaction, he glanced at Stark and said, "I think I'd better go through everything that was left in Juan's shack, just to make sure we haven't missed anything."

Stark nodded. "That's a good idea. I don't reckon he had much, but you never know what you'll find." He grunted and shook his head. "Nobody ever expected to find that land grant, that's for sure. Turning it up was an accident, pure and simple."

"Yep." Chadwick took the receipt the teller handed him, then turned to Stark and went on, "I've got to go back to the office first. Why don't we meet over at the shack later and go through Juan's effects?"

Stark thought that over, then nodded. "I reckon it would be a good idea if I was there, all right. That way folks'll know everything's on the up and up. Not that anybody'd figure otherwise."

"I know what you mean," Chadwick assured him. "See you there in a little while?"

"Sure. I may go on over in a few minutes and start looking around."

"Fine." Chadwick tucked the receipt away and left with a casual wave.

Stark followed him out of the bank and turned toward the side street where Juan's shack was located. He had heard a great deal about the dilapidated old hovel since arriving in Garrison, but he hadn't actually seen the place. It wasn't likely anything else would turn up that would have any bearing on the case, but you could never tell about these things. So much had happened already that no one could ever have anticipated.

That was what made the law interesting, Stark reflected. Laws themselves might be cut and dried, even boring, but the folks they affected seldom were.

Take Juan Espina. At one time, the family he belonged to had been prominent enough to receive a land grant from the king of Spain. What had old Emiliano Espina done that made the king grateful enough to give him such a valuable gift? Had he been a statesman, or a soldier, or maybe a friend to royalty? Stark had no way of knowing. Maybe somewhere, across the sea in Spain itself, the truth lay written in some book moldering in the royal archives, but Stark would never read it.

And what had happened to the Espina family along the way, he wondered, to bring them to the point where the last surviving member was a drunken, poverty-stricken old man? That was another question that could never be answered with any certainty. Even if Juan had known, he was dead and would soon be buried, and any answers he possessed would be buried with him.

Stark turned onto the side street, walked a couple of blocks, and spotted the shack. He knew right away he had found the right place; none of the other dwellings in Garrison looked quite so disreputable.

The shack was leaning so much it seemed as if a strong breeze would topple it. The roof sagged almost to the point of collapse, and the walls were full of gaping holes. Only the relatively mild climate of this area made the hovel inhabitable. Stark let out a long sigh. It was ironic that Juan Espina, who overnight had become one of the wealthiest men in the territory, had lived in such appalling poverty.

The door, barely hanging by its rusty hinges, was closed. Stark pushed it open carefully so that it didn't fall completely off, then stepped inside. The bright morning sunshine that came through the open door and the holes in the roof was sufficient to light up the interior.

There wasn't much to see. Stark glanced at the bunk and the three-legged table that leaned to one side. Matt Curry had found the old Bible containing the land grant papers under the table, Stark recalled. No one had cleaned the place since Juan had left, so empty tequila bottles and dried tortilla husks still littered the dirt floor.

In his excitement over finding the land grant, Curry had failed to search any further; there had been no reason for him to do so. As Stark's gaze fell on the ancient trunk, he saw that no one had touched it since that fateful day, either. A coating of dust still lay thick on the old, cracked leather.

Stark knelt in front of the trunk. The lid had a simple clasp holding it down. He unfastened it and lifted the lid, the hinges squealing in protest as he did. Dust flew in the air.

Stark batted his free hand back and forth in front of his face, then leaned forward to peer into the trunk. The first thing he saw was some black rags that on closer examination proved to be the remains of a suit. He figured the outfit had belonged to Juan, but the old man hadn't had any reason to wear it for a long time, and bugs had gotten to it. There were more empty tequila bottles in the trunk, too. Juan seemed to have owned more of them than anything else.

With a grunt Stark moved some of the bottles and

The Diablo Grant

the pile of rags aside. He was convinced that he wasn't going to find anything the least bit interesting, but since Juan was dead, somebody had to go through his effects. He dug his hands down a little deeper.

His fingers touched leather, and he heard a soft clinking sound. Eyes widening, he took hold of the item and pulled it out. It was a small pouch, closed at the top with a drawstring. From its weight and the noises coming from inside it, Stark had a pretty good idea what it contained, although he was certainly surprised by the discovery.

He opened the pouch and upended it. Coins spilled out into his palm, gold and silver coins that gleamed dully in the filtered sunlight. Stark began counting, and a frown appeared on his face.

There was hardly enough money here for Juan to have considered himself wealthy, or even comfortable. But there was sure more than Stark had expected to find. He had been told that Juan usually had enough coins to buy a bottle of liquor, and this was obviously the cache from which the money came. But where had Juan gotten the coins in the first place? There was more here than he could have earned doing an occasional— *very* occasional, from what Stark had heard—odd job.

His curiosity aroused, Stark replaced the coins in the pouch and set it aside, then delved deeper into the old trunk. He had found one surprise already, so who was to say he might not find another? His fingers closed around something else, and he brought it out: a small book not much larger than the palm of his hand.

Stark opened the book, being careful not to tear the yellowed, crackling pages. The first half of the book was filled with writing so faded that he could not make out the words, except to discern that they were written in Spanish. From the ancient feel of the book, he decided the writing might be a hundred years old or more.

But about midway through the volume the ink darkened suddenly, which suggested to Stark that the writing here was much more recent. He recognized Juan Espina's hand. After a quick flip through the pages he ascertained that more than a dozen of them were covered with Juan's spidery scrawl. He turned back to where Juan's writing began, figuring that he would try to translate it. If he couldn't, he reckoned Billy Chadwick probably could.

Before Stark could begin reading, a footstep sounded behind him at the entrance to the shack. Thinking that Chadwick had arrived, Stark started to stand up and turn around to greet him.

"Look what I found in this old trunk, Billy—" he began.

That was as far as he got before he saw a flicker of motion from the corner of his eye and something slammed into the side of his head. Stark had been pistol-whipped before, and in the small part of his stunned brain that was still working he figured that was what had happened to him now. He tried to stay upright, but another blow crashed into his skull, sending him sprawling on the hard-packed dirt floor. The world spun crazily out of control around him. He was vaguely aware of hearing another footstep.

And that was the last sound he heard for a while as darkness welled up, covered him, and pulled him down in its steely grip.

Reluctantly, Stark came back to the land of the living. The black nothingness that enfolded him was so much more comforting than the realm of pain and confusion beyond.

But somebody was shaking him insistently, and a familiar voice was saying, "Judge! Judge Stark! Are you all right?"

Stark groaned and winced as consciousness seeped back into his brain. Another familiar voice said excitedly, "He's coming around!"

Billy Chadwick was looming over him and shaking him, Stark saw as he forced his eyes open. Matt Curry and Angelina Montoya were both in the shack, too, peering anxiously over Chadwick's shoulders. Stark blinked and tried to lift his head, then let it fall back as he realized what a mistake that was.

"You'd better take it easy, Judge," Chadwick told him. "Looks like you took quite a clout on the head."

"A couple of 'em," Stark rasped. "I reckon it wasn't you who hit me, Counselor?"

"I just got here," Chadwick replied with a shake of his head. "Matt and Señorita Montoya came by my office to talk to me about Dolores, and I asked them to come over here with me."

Stark focused on Curry. "You know about Dolores and Juan's will?"

The editor nodded. "She came to the newspaper office to ask me what she should do about it. She's really upset about everything."

Stark managed to nod, and this time the movement didn't set off explosions behind his eyes. He decided to try sitting up again.

With Chadwick's help he got upright and lifted a hand to his throbbing head. He felt a patch of sticky wetness in the thinning hair above his left ear, then steeled himself to the pain and explored the actual wound with his fingertips. A good-sized goose egg was forming, topped by a gash that had probably been torn by the sight of the gun that had hit him. His vision was clear, though, and the nausea he had felt when he first woke up was abating now. Stark decided that he wasn't badly hurt; he had just been knocked out. This wasn't the first time that had happened.

"Wonder how long I was out," he muttered.

"Couldn't have been long," Chadwick said. "It's only been about forty-five minutes since we left the bank."

"You didn't see anybody leaving here when you came up?"

Chadwick shook his head. "Not a soul."

Matt Curry asked, "Did you see who did this to you, Your Honor?"

"Nope, it all happened too fast. I was kneeling down in front of that trunk over there"—Stark gestured toward the still-open trunk—"when I heard somebody come in. Figured it was you, Billy, so I started to stand up and turn around. That's when somebody walloped me with a gun. I never even caught a good glimpse of him, the no-good—"

Out of respect for Señorita Montoya, Stark bit off the stream of curses that had almost escaped his lips. Turning the air blue wasn't going to help anything, anyway. He looked around the shack, which took only a second, and the glance confirmed what he already suspected.

"The book and the money are gone," he said heavily.

Billy Chadwick peered closely at him. "What book and money?"

"I found a pouch of coins in that trunk," Stark said,

gesturing again. "And there was a little book in there, too. I couldn't tell what it was. Most of the writing in it was old, real old. But there were a few pages where Juan had written something." He grimaced. "I never got a chance to figure out what it was. Somebody knocked me out before I could read it."

Curry began, "But who—"

"I don't know," Stark cut in. "But it sure as blazes wasn't Cord Richmond. He's still locked up, unless Sheriff Higgins has taken leave of his senses."

"I'm certain Cord's still in jail," Chadwick said. "Anyway, he wouldn't have any reason for doing something like this."

"Help me up," Stark said. "I want to take a look around."

Curry suggested, "Maybe one of us ought to go get the doctor to take a look at your head, Judge Stark."

"I've been knocked out before, son," Stark told him with a touch of impatience. "Now give me a hand here, unless you want me to get up by myself and maybe fall on my face again."

Chadwick gave a grim chuckle. "We'd better not argue with the judge, Matt. I reckon he knows his own head better than anybody else."

"Darn right," Stark snapped.

Chadwick and Curry got on either side of him, took hold of his arms, and lifted him to his feet. Stark stood there and shook his head like an old bull, clearing away the last of the cobwebs. Curry and Chadwick stepped back, and although Stark was unsteady on his feet for a few seconds, the feeling passed quickly. He peered down at the tracks on the floor of the shack. The dirt didn't hold prints well because it was packed down so hard, and what few marks Stark could make out were a meaningless jumble.

"I've known a few trackers who might be able to make some sense out of that mess," Stark said, "but I'm not one of 'em."

"Besides, we trampled over any prints that might've been there," Chadwick pointed out. "I'm afraid you're not going to find many clues as to who might've clouted you, Judge."

"I'll find out," Stark grunted. "One way or another, I'll find out."

He didn't take kindly to being knocked out like that, and it was clear that whoever had attacked him had been after either the book, the pouch of coins, or both. There hadn't been enough money in the pouch to make robbery worthwhile, so Stark figured the little book was the key. He wished he'd had time to read what Juan had written in it.

"Come on," he told the others. "We'd better tell the sheriff about this."

"Wait a minute," Chadwick said. "Was there anything else in that trunk?"

"Just some old rags and empty tequila bottles." Stark went over to the trunk and pawed through its contents one last time. "Nope, that's it, all right."

With Chadwick and Curry flanking him in case he got woozy again, Stark led the way out of the shack and back to Garrison's main street. He turned toward the sheriff's office, but Boone Higgins appeared before Stark and his companions got there, hurrying out with an agitated-looking Edmund Wells behind him.

The Diablo Grant

The sheriff spotted Stark and the others marching resolutely toward him, and he loped forward to meet them.

"Reckon you must've heard," Higgins said. "I'll be gettin' up a posse right now. You gents want to ride along with us?"

"What the devil are you talking about, Sheriff?" demanded Stark. "Did somebody see who attacked me?"

Higgins blinked in confusion. "Somebody bushwhacked you, Judge? This is the first I've heard of it."

Stark touched the lump on the side of his head. "I was down at Juan Espina's old shack just now, when somebody jumped me and pistol-whipped me. What are *you* talking about, Sheriff?"

"Why, about that gal Dolores bein' kidnapped, of course!" Higgins jerked a blunt thumb at the banker. "Mr. Wells here saw 'em ridin' out of town with her."

"That's right," Wells said, mopping sweat off his forehead with a handkerchief. "The young woman was struggling and seemed quite agitated. One of the men with her clapped a hand over her mouth to keep her from crying out, and then they practically threw her on the back of a horse and galloped out of town with her."

"How many men grabbed her?" Stark asked sharply, thinking about the will that had given ownership of the Diablo Valley to Dolores. That made her valuable, indeed.

"About half a dozen. They were dressed like cowhands, but I didn't recognize any of them. They were quite rough-looking, like they might have been outlaws."

"Hired hardcases, more'n likely," the sheriff said. "Well, come on. I got to round up some deputies and get a posse mounted."

"Wait a minute," Stark said. "Mr. Wells, where did this happen?"

"I saw them in the alley behind the hotel," the banker replied. "They must have taken the young woman out the rear door and had their horses waiting back there. I was just walking down the street when I spotted the commotion." Wells was pale. "One of the men drew his gun, and for a moment I thought he was going to shoot at me. It was awful. But then they rode off. I suppose they didn't want to add murder to kidnapping—thank God!"

Stark nodded his thanks to the banker, then said to Higgins, "I'll ride with you, Sheriff. You probably don't realize it yet, but Dolores is very important."

"I'd go after any gal that got hauled off like that, but what're you talkin' about, Judge?"

Stark exchanged a quick glance with Chadwick and Curry. There was no point in keeping the will a secret now, since it seemed to Stark that somebody already knew about it. Otherwise there would have been no reason to abduct Dolores.

"She's the new owner of Diablo Valley," Stark said. "Now let's go, Sheriff. Those scoundrels've already got a big enough lead on us."

Curry turned to the young woman beside him and said quickly, "You'd better tell your father about this, Angelina. He may want to come with us, too." Then he hurried down the street after Stark, Chadwick, and Sheriff Higgins, who were heading for the livery stable to fetch their horses.

The Diablo Grant

Edmund Wells stared after them and said, "Did . . . did Judge Stark say that young woman now owns the Diablo Valley?"

"That is right, Señor Wells. Now, you must excuse me." Angelina hurried off in search of Don Alfonso.

Wells shook his head and wiped more sweat off his brow. This part of the territory was in an uproar the likes of which it had never seen before.

And it didn't look as if things were going to settle down anytime soon, either.

Chapter Twelve

It didn't take long to get a posse together. Acting on Stark's advice, Higgins left his regular deputies at the jail to guard Cord Richmond—in case Dolores's kidnapping was a ruse to lure the authorities out of town—and swore in several townsmen as members of the posse, along with Stark, Chadwick, and Curry. Don Alfonso Montoya arrived shortly thereafter, bringing with him a couple of the bodyguards who had accompanied him from Mexico City.

"I wish to come with you, Sheriff," the Mexican diplomat said as he hurried up to the group gathering in front of the livery stable. "It is in the best interests of my government that this young woman be rescued from her captors. My daughter tells me that she is the heir of Juan Espina."

The Diablo Grant

"That's right," Higgins replied, "and I reckon it's all right if you come along, Don Alfonso. You got to realize, though, it's liable to be dangerous."

"I own a *rancho* in the north of Mexico, señor. In my time I have defended it from *bandidos,* Apaches, and Yaqui renegades. Despite my current position as a representative of *Presídente* Diaz, I am no stranger to trouble."

Looking at the old boy, Stark was willing to bet that was the truth, all right. Don Alfonso's dark eyes were narrowed and glittering with anger.

"Sure, come ahead, and we'll be glad to have you," the sheriff told Montoya. "I figure we'll need all the guns we can get."

Five minutes later the posse was mounted and galloped out of Garrison, the horses' hooves clattering on the planks of a bridge that crossed a small creek just north of town. That was the way the kidnappers had gone, according to Edmund Wells. The trail, which led north to the ranches of Diablo Valley, was fairly well traveled, but as Stark rode along in the lead with Sheriff Higgins, he could make out the tracks of a large group of riders that had passed that way recently.

It didn't appear as if the kidnappers had tried to hide their trail. Several miles north of Garrison, they had veered off the road and struck out across open rangeland, but their tracks were still easy to follow.

Stark said to Higgins, "Where do you reckon they're going? What's out this way?"

"Looks like they may be headin' for White Horse Pass," the lawman replied. "That ain't the main way into Diablo Valley, but it gets there just the same. The road goes through another pass where the country ain't quite so rugged."

Stark had noticed that the terrain was getting a little steeper and rougher, culminating in a low range of hills up ahead that no doubt marked one side of Diablo Valley. As Higgins suspected, the tracks led to a narrow gap in the hills. The approach was rocky, and the path twisted and turned.

That pass might not be a bad spot for an ambush, Stark found himself thinking; the kidnappers could have left a few men there to slow down any pursuit. He scanned the hills on either side of the gap intently as the posse rode closer.

He saw no signs of movement, and if gunmen were hiding there, they were taking pains to keep the sunlight from reflecting off their rifle barrels. Nevertheless Stark said, "Maybe we'd better not go charging through there until we're sure nobody's waiting to give us a reception."

"That's a good idea," Billy Chadwick chimed in. "I'll ride through the pass first and take a look around."

"No, you won't, Mr. Chadwick," Higgins said. "I'm in charge of this here posse, so I reckon that chore oughta be mine. You boys slow up and hang back until I tell you to come on."

The sheriff spurred his horse ahead of the others and rode at a brisk trot toward the pass. Stark's first impulse was to go with him, but he decided to honor the sheriff's wishes and pulled the big Appaloosa back to a slow walk as Higgins drew ahead. The other possemen followed suit.

"This Palouse of mine doesn't like for anybody else

The Diablo Grant

to get out in front," Stark commented as his mount shook its head impatiently.

Chadwick laughed. "I imagine the horse isn't the only one."

Stark grinned and shrugged. "I never cared for asking somebody to run a risk I wouldn't run myself."

"But you would have gone first, and everybody here knows it. You don't have to prove anything, Judge."

Stark shrugged again and turned his gaze back to the trail ahead. Sheriff Higgins was riding through the pass now, and so far nothing had happened. He reached the other side, reined in, and looked around, studying the rocks and crevices closely. Then he turned back to the posse, lifted an arm, and waved them ahead.

"Looks like the way's clear," Chadwick said.

Stark didn't waste any breath replying; he heeled the Appaloosa into a trot again.

Moments later the posse joined Higgins on the far side of the pass. The kidnappers' tracks had disappeared; the ground here was too rocky to show hoofprints. But as the ground sloped down on the other side of the pass and turned into the long, green, pine-dotted valley that was home to several prosperous ranches, the trail reappeared.

Higgins gestured at the tracks. "They came through here, all right," he said. "I'm pretty sure it's the same bunch."

Stark was convinced of that, too. "Whose spread are we on now?" he asked.

"Travis Richmond's," Chadwick told him. "Antlers runs all the way up this side of the valley. Ben Tompkins's Boxed BT is on the other side, and the smaller spreads are up at the north end. The main road goes down the center of the valley, and it's the dividing line between Richmond's place and Tompkins's."

"But you could cut across Richmond's spread to get to the Boxed BT?"

"Sure," Chadwick said. "You think Tompkins had something to do with grabbing Dolores?"

"I don't know who's behind it," Stark replied honestly. "Might not have been any of the ranchers. Let's follow these tracks and see if we can find out."

After a quarter-hour of riding, Sheriff Higgins commented, "You know, if I didn't know better, I'd say those boys're headed for Trav Richmond's old place."

"What do you mean?" Stark asked.

Billy Chadwick provided the explanation. "When Richmond first started Antlers, a long time ago, he didn't use the ranch house he has for his headquarters now. That place wasn't even built yet. He told me once about how he built a log cabin with his own hands, and that was how Antlers got its start. Named the ranch after some antlers from a deer he shot that first winter. He put the horns above the door of that old cabin. Then later, after the ranch was established, he got married, and of course he had to have a better house for his wife."

"The hands used the old place as a line shack for a spell," Higgins put in, "but I think it's been deserted for quite a while now."

Stark thought about what he had been told and nodded. "Sounds like a good place for somebody to hole up," he said, adding grimly, "Especially if Richmond had anything to do with kidnapping Dolores."

Chadwick said, "I hate to think that he would do

something like that, but I suppose if he was pushed far enough—"

"Like being faced not only with maybe losing his ranch but the possibility that his only son might be convicted of murder and hanged?"

Chadwick nodded. "I reckon that might do it, all right."

A few minutes later the old log cabin, the original headquarters of the Antlers ranch, came into view. It sat on the edge of a wide meadow, surrounded by a huge expanse of open ground on three sides. A thicket of pines ran almost to the rear of the cabin.

At a command from Higgins, the members of the posse reined up on the far side of the meadow while the sheriff, Chadwick, and Stark studied the cabin. There were no horses in front of the building, but they could have been hidden out back among the trees. Nor was there any smoke coming from the stone chimney. But that didn't necessarily mean anything, either—it was a warm day, warm enough that the kidnappers wouldn't need a fire for heat, and under the circumstances it was doubtful they would need one for cooking. At any rate, the tracks the posse had been following led across the meadow straight toward the cabin.

"I'd be willin' to bet they're in there, even if we can't see 'em," Higgins said as he leaned forward in the saddle.

Stark nodded. "I agree. Maybe we'd better circle around this meadow and try to come up behind the cabin—"

Before he could finish his suggestion a bullet buzzed past his ear, followed a split second later by the whipcrack of a rifle. Stark spat out a curse as Higgins shouted, "Ever'body get back! Fall back into them trees!"

The possemen wheeled their horses and drove them deeper into the pines as more shots came from the cabin, and bullets sang through the air around them. One of the townsmen let out a howl of pain as a slug burned his shoulder. His arm hung limp, and he sagged in the saddle as he guided his mount into the cover of the trees.

Stark slid down from the Appaloosa, pulling his Winchester from the saddleboot as he did. A sharp slap on the big horse's rump sent it trotting deeper into the pines. Stark ran back to the edge of the trees and dropped to a crouch behind one of the thicker trunks. He saw powder smoke drifting from the windows and the door of the cabin, which was now open.

Billy Chadwick and Sheriff Higgins joined Stark, seeking cover behind trees at the edge of the woods. The lawyer called over to Stark, "Reckon that cinches it. They're in there, all right."

Higgins lifted his rifle. "I can put some lead through that door they got open—"

"Forget about it, Sheriff," Stark cut in. "If the kidnappers are in there, so is Dolores, and if we get a bunch of slugs ricocheting around, she'll get hit for sure." He looked around. The other men had dismounted and found cover behind the trees, except for Matt Curry. Twisting his head, Stark looked over his shoulder and saw that the young newspaperman had halted deeper in the woods. He was holding the reins of the horses, keeping the nervous animals under control. That was a good job for him, Stark thought.

Don Alfonso had moved up alongside the sheriff,

The Diablo Grant

and he asked, "What are we going to do now, señores?"

Higgins looked at Stark, and the judge realized he was being deferred to. "We'd best make sure what we're dealing with first," Stark said. He lifted his voice and shouted over the sporadic shots coming from the cabin, "Hold your fire! Hold your fire, damn it! Who's in there?"

"None o' your damn business!" came a shout in return. "All you got to know is that we got that Mex gal in here, and we'll kill her if'n you don't do like we say!"

Stark didn't recognize the voice. No doubt a hired gun, like the man who had tried to steal the land grant papers from his hotel room. Which meant that he was none too trustworthy. Stark called back, "How do we know you have Dolores?"

"Just listen up!"

A scream ripped from the cabin then, a scream more of terror than of pain, and there was no doubt it came from a woman. Several of the possemen cursed, and Matt Curry called anxiously, "That sounds like Dolores, Judge!"

"I reckon they've got her, all right," Stark muttered. "That scream sounded like she's still healthy enough, though—for now, anyway."

"Reckon we could work our way around behind that cabin?" Higgins asked.

"We could, but it'll take a while, and I'm sure they've got men watching in that direction, too." Stark frowned darkly, trying to figure out what to do next. This was precisely the kind of predicament he hated.

They could start by establishing what the kidnappers wanted. He raised his voice again and called,

"Don't hurt the girl! What is it you want in return for her safety?"

"You that judge, the one called Big Earl?"

Stark didn't waste time explaining that he hadn't been known by that name for a long time. "Yeah!" he shouted.

"Then you know what we want! Let Cord Richmond go, and the girl lives!"

Stark exchanged glances with Higgins, Billy Chadwick, and Don Alfonso. "Sounds like Richmond's behind this, all right," he said. "He probably doesn't even know about Juan's will. He just figured Dolores would serve as a good bargaining chip to get his son back."

Chadwick nodded solemnly. "I hate to think Travis Richmond would stoop this low, but I don't suppose there's much doubt now. He wants his son back, and he's willing to go to any lengths to get him."

"I can't let a killer go," Higgins said. "Even if he ain't been tried and convicted yet, Cord's still my prisoner."

"And I don't want to ask you to let him go, Sheriff," Stark said. "But we can't let Dolores be murdered, either."

Don Alfonso put in, "This man Richmond—he might hire men to kidnap the girl, but would he actually have her killed?"

"None of us would like to think so," Chadwick said. "But I'd hate to bet somebody's life on that opinion. And that's what we'd be doing if we rushed the cabin."

"Not to mention that those fellas'd pick off a good number of us," Stark said. "No, there's got to be a better way." He thought for a moment, then came to a decision. "Sheriff, you and your men stay here. Keep

The Diablo Grant

those gents in the cabin bottled up. Billy, Don Alfonso, we'll ride over to Richmond's headquarters and see if he's there. We haven't heard anything from him, and if he was with that bunch, I reckon he'd be doing his own negotiating."

"He may be holed up at the ranch house with more gunmen in case there's trouble," Chadwick warned.

"Then that'll tell us he's really behind this," Stark said. "I'm not completely convinced of that yet." He jerked his head toward the horses. "Come on."

As they slipped back through the trees to the spot where Matt Curry was tending to the horses, more slugs came flying from the cabin, clipping branches and bark from the trees. Stark wasn't sure if they were actually trying to hit anything or were simply keeping the whole hornet's nest stirred up so that the law would know they meant business.

"I heard what you're doing," Curry said as he handed over the reins of their mounts. "I'm coming with you."

Stark nodded. "Come ahead. It may not be any safer where we're going, though."

"I don't care about that. If Travis Richmond is behind this, I want to be there when you confront him."

Stark swung up into the Appaloosa's saddle. "Let's ride, then," he said as he jammed his Winchester back into the boot.

Billy Chadwick, who was more familiar with the layout of the valley than Curry was, led the way. It took a little over an hour of hard riding before the four men came in sight of the big ranch house.

Everything around the ranch headquarters looked normal as the riders approached. Smoke was drifting up from the chimney of the cook shack, where the cookie was no doubt preparing a midday meal for the punchers who would soon be coming back in from the range. The ringing of hammer against steel sounded from the small blacksmith shop. A few cowboys were leaning on the fence around a corral where a bronc buster was knocking the last rough edges off a big sorrel.

From this distance the sound of the shooting around the old log cabin wasn't audible, so the men who were here would have no inkling that any sort of trouble was going on—unless they were part of Richmond's plan to free his son. As the riders came up to the yard in front of the house, Stark glanced at the others and said, "I'll do the talking, since I'm the only one here with any authority."

"Suits me," Chadwick said. Curry and Montoya agreed.

"Hello the house!" Stark called out. "You in there, Richmond?"

There was no response from the house, but the cowboys who had been watching the bronc buster at work came over, their faces hardening when they saw who the visitors were.

"Howdy, Judge," one of them said with a nod, obviously forcing himself to be civil. "What can we do for you?"

"We're looking for Travis Richmond," Stark said.

The lean, middle-aged puncher shook his head. "He ain't here. Rode out early this mornin', said he was goin' to Garrison to see his boy." His eyes narrowed. "No offense, Judge, but you was wrong to throw Cord in jail for killin' that old man. Cord flies off the handle easy sometimes, but he ain't no killer."

The Diablo Grant

"That's for the law to decide," Stark said. "Was Richmond by himself when he left?"

"Yep, he sure was. How come you're askin' all these questions, Judge?"

"There's been a little trouble," Stark replied tersely. His instincts told him the expressions of bafflement on the faces of the cowboys were genuine. Richmond hadn't told these men what he was planning.

But he *had* told them he was going to town to see his son. It seemed likely to Stark that Richmond had had *something* in mind when he started for Garrison—such as kidnapping Dolores and trading her for Cord, perhaps.

"What sort of trouble?" the older cowboy asked sharply.

"That's our business, I'm afraid."

All the cowboys were getting more hostile by the second. Several of them tensed and moved their hands closer to the guns on their hips.

"We don't much like what you done to the boss or to Cord," said the older man. "I reckon you best get off Antlers, and take these other fellas with you, Judge."

"We're going," Stark replied. "But if you see Richmond, you tell him we're looking for him."

One of the younger men spat contemptuously. "We ain't passin' on any messages for the likes of you. Now git!"

Stark glanced at Chadwick and Montoya. Being addressed that way clearly didn't sit well with them, and Stark didn't like it, either. But right now there were more important considerations than wounded pride.

As he pulled the Appaloosa's head around, he

grunted, "Come on." He and his companions rode away from the ranch.

"You believe those boys?" Chadwick asked when they were out of earshot of the cowboys.

Stark nodded. "Reckon I do. Richmond wouldn't want to get any of his regular hands in trouble with the law, I imagine, even though they would have gone into town and broken Cord out of jail if he'd asked them to. He must've hired men especially for this chore, men who wouldn't mind kidnapping a woman. That means they probably wouldn't mind killing her, either."

Curry asked, "Then where's Mr. Richmond now?"

Stark had to shake his head. "Don't know. Could be he's lying low until it's all over, or he could be in town waiting for us to come back and release Cord in order to trade him for Dolores."

"Either way, there's still no good solution," Chadwick said.

Stark shrugged. The lawyer was right, and no amount of discussion was going to change that.

"Let's head back to the cabin," Stark said. "Maybe we can talk sense into whoever's in charge in there."

"You're not counting on that, are you?" Chadwick asked.

"I'm not counting on anything," Stark said bluntly, "except the fact that this is probably the most frustrating mess I've ever gotten mixed up in."

They pushed their horses even harder on the way back to the old ranch headquarters, covering the distance in a little less than an hour. When they were within a mile of the place, they heard shots again.

The Diablo Grant

"Sounds like they're still at it," Matt Curry said, a distinct undertone of worry in his voice.

"That's good," Stark told him. "If it was quiet, that would mean things were all over. And if that was the case, there'd be just as good a chance that the outcome was bad."

The shots came at a desultory, irregular pace, and Stark realized that the siege was dragging on longer than anyone had expected. Folks tired quickly under the stress of a situation such as this one, when every second that ticked by brought another chance of sudden death. Sometimes that tension could work in favor of a peaceful settlement, but just as often it led to a desperate, bloody attempt to break the stalemate. Stark hoped that Sheriff Higgins and the posse kept their wits about them.

There was a sudden flurry of shots as Stark and his companions reached the band of trees that marked one edge of the meadow where the cabin was located. The gunfire intensified rather than dying down again, and Stark knew something was badly wrong. He rode quickly through the trees, ignoring the branches that slapped at him, and dropped out of the saddle only when he spotted Sheriff Higgins up ahead. The lawman was standing behind a pine tree, cussing a blue streak.

"What happened, blast it?" Stark demanded as he ran up. Chadwick, Curry, and Don Alfonso followed closely behind him. Out in the meadow Stark could see a dozen or more riders charging toward the cabin, laying down a barrage of fire from horseback and running into an equally withering hail of lead.

"It's Tompkins!" the sheriff yelled. "That crazy son

of a buck heard about the stunt Richmond's tryin' to pull, and he brought his men to try and flush those hardcases out of the cabin!"

"Tompkins!" Stark exclaimed in surprise. "I thought he and Richmond were working together."

"They've always hated each other," Chadwick said grimly. "I figured their truce was just a temporary one. Tompkins grabbed the first opportunity he found to turn on Richmond again."

"Damn it," Stark grated as he looked past the sheriff at the pitched battle going on now in the meadow. Some of Tompkins's men had already fallen to the kidnappers' bullets, but the rest were still charging, pouring lead at the old cabin. Dolores was in there, and she'd die for sure in this chaos.

Stark wheeled around and ran for his horse.

"Judge! Where are you going?" Chadwick called after him.

"I'm going to save that girl," Stark shouted over his shoulder as he grabbed the saddlehorn and swung up.

Chapter Thirteen

As Stark jabbed his bootheels in the Appaloosa's flanks and sent the horse lunging forward in a gallop, he heard Sheriff Higgins bellowing to the posse behind him, "Follow Tompkins and his boys! We ain't got no choice now!"

That was right, Stark thought. One way or another, the standoff was over. Now things would have to be settled with smoke and blood and death.

He glanced over his shoulder and saw Billy Chadwick riding after him. Curry and Don Alfonso were hanging back, out of the fight, and Stark was glad of that. The young newspaperman was out of his element here, and although the diplomat could probably handle himself all right, if he got killed it could lead to an international incident with Mexico. Stark didn't want that. But he was glad to have Chadwick backing his play.

Instead of riding straight toward the cabin, Stark swung wide around the edge of the meadow. As he did, he saw from the corner of his eye that Tompkins and his men were finally breaking off their charge, peeling away in the face of the unrelenting gunfire from the cabin. They could regroup and attack again, however, and that was exactly what Stark expected them to do.

Meanwhile, Stark was heading for the back of the old log building. Those inside would probably be ready for him, but with any luck the frontal attack would distract the cabin's defenders long enough to give him a chance.

Guns began banging again as Stark circled the meadow and rode hard for the rear of the cabin. Chadwick was still a few yards behind him. A quick glance told Stark that the punchers from the Boxed BT were once again attacking the cabin, their ranks bolstered this time by the posse from Garrison. Stark leaned forward in the saddle, urging all possible speed out of the Appaloosa. As he neared the cabin, he switched the reins to his left hand and pulled the LeMat from its holster with his right.

There was a back door to the place, Stark could see now. It flew open, and smoke and flame streaked from the shadowy interior as he flung himself out of the saddle, landed on his feet, and started running. The slug fanned by his head as he triggered a shot in return, aiming at the muzzle flash. He heard a man howl in pain.

Then Stark was in the doorway, diving through, his hat flying off as he rolled and then came up in a crouch, his eyes searching for a new target. Despite the deaf-

The Diablo Grant

ening roar of guns, he could hear hooves clattering outside the front door.

Stark's eyesight, like all his senses, was keenest in these frozen moments of time when death lurked just around the corner. His gaze flicked around the single room of the cabin and came to rest on an unexpected sight: Travis Richmond was lying sprawled on the dirt floor, the front of his shirt stained with blood and his eyes staring glassily at the beamed ceiling. The rancher was dead.

Next to him was Dolores, and she was very much alive, although tied hand and foot and shrieking with horror as she wriggled futilely against her bonds. Standing over her was a roughly dressed man with hard, drawn, beard-stubbled features. He had a gun in his hand, and he was swinging it toward Dolores.

The other kidnappers were already dead, scattered around the room in bloody heaps. The lone gunman's lips were drawn back in a snarl as he brought his revolver to bear on the helpless captive.

Stark saw all of that in a heartbeat, a whisker of time, as his own gun came up. At the same instant a burly figure appeared in the front door of the cabin, also carrying a gun. Ben Tompkins must have taken in the scene as quickly as Stark had, because his pistol roared at the same time the LeMat bucked and blasted in Stark's hand.

The judge's bullet took the kidnapper in the chest and drove him toward the front of the cabin as another slug kicked up dust beside Dolores's head. The hardcase landed heavily on his back, kicked a couple of times spasmodically, then lay still, his pistol slipping from nerveless fingers.

It had all happened almost blindingly fast, but Stark's instincts screamed a warning at him that something was still wrong. An instant later he knew what he had witnessed.

But that slight hesitation was enough to allow Ben Tompkins to swing the barrel of his revolver toward Stark. The cattleman's face was contorted with hate as he rasped, "Too bad you got killed in the fightin', too, Judge."

Stark flung himself to the side as Tompkins fired. At the same time, another gun went off behind Stark, the sound of it merging with Tompkins's shot. The rancher wasn't hit, but he was forced to dart to the side, which threw off his own aim. From the floor Stark thumbed off a shot from the LeMat, and the slug ripped through Tompkins's shoulder. The impact threw him back and spun him around. Billy Chadwick, who had fired the shot that distracted Tompkins, dashed across the room and kicked the gun out of the rancher's hand.

As he trained his own weapon on the fallen Tompkins, Chadwick said, "I don't know what's going on here, but I just saw you try to murder Judge Stark, Tompkins. If you make another move, I'll kill you."

"He won't try anything else," Stark said as he climbed to his feet. "I reckon he knows it's all over."

Dolores had stopped screaming. For a second, as he looked at her pale features and the way her head lolled limply on her shoulders, Stark thought she had caught a bullet after all. But then he knelt beside her and with his fingers found the pulse in her throat, and he knew she had just fainted. Well, she had good cause, Stark mused; she had come about as close to death as anybody could.

The Diablo Grant

Sheriff Higgins and the other members of the posse, along with some of Tompkins's men, came boiling into the small cabin. Higgins took one look at Travis Richmond's dead features and cursed bitterly. "Looks like Richmond was behind all this after all," he said. "I was sort of hopin' maybe he wasn't."

"He wasn't," Stark said as he glanced up from where he was kneeling beside Dolores. "He was as much a victim as this young woman."

"What're you talkin' about, Judge?"

Stark stood up. As a couple of Tompkins's men hauled their wounded boss to his feet, Stark said sharply, "Better stand back. Tompkins is under arrest for kidnapping and attempted murder."

"What the hell are you talkin' about?" Tompkins snarled. "Me and my boys just came over here to help out when we heard what Richmond had done!"

Stark shook his head. "It won't wash, Tompkins. Billy and I both heard you threaten me, and I saw you try to kill Dolores so there would be no chance she could ever implicate you. You couldn't be sure what she might have overheard while she was a prisoner, so you had to get rid of her."

"You're crazy!" Tompkins insisted. "I tried to save her from that fella!"

"Your bullet kicked up dust right beside her head. I reckon you hurried your shot a little. You weren't shooting at that hardcase at all. It was *my* slug that put him down."

Tompkins shook his head. "*He* was the one who shot at the girl."

"He didn't get a shot off," Stark cut in. "I saw that plain as day."

"Then maybe you missed and *I* was the one who got

the son of a bitch." Tompkins was grasping his wounded shoulder and scowling in pain, but he kept arguing desperately.

"He fell *toward* you, Tompkins. And he's hit in the chest, but his back was to the door where you came in. There's no doubt about what happened. I saw all of it, but it took me a second to figure out what it meant. By then you were trying to kill *me*. I reckon if you had, you'd have blamed it on that hardcase, said he got me with his dying shot."

The cattleman's face twisted again, and everyone in the room could see that Stark's accusation had hit home. Even Tompkins's own men moved away from him a little as the truth of Stark's words sank in.

"But why?" Higgins wanted to know. "I still don't understand all of this."

Before Stark could explain the theory that was still coming together in his head, Matt Curry and Don Alfonso appeared in the doorway. Curry rushed over to Dolores and exclaimed, "My God, is she—"

"She'll be all right, son," Stark told him. "She's just passed out from the strain she's been under."

"I'll see if I can bring her around," Curry said as he knelt beside Dolores's senseless form and took one of her hands in both of his. Don Alfonso moved around to the young woman's other side.

While they were doing that, Stark inclined his head toward the door, and the rest of the men moved outside into the afternoon sunlight. Higgins got to work patching up the wound in Tompkins's shoulder, bandaging it so that it wouldn't bleed too much on the ride back to town. Stark continued with his explanation.

The Diablo Grant

"The way I see it, Tompkins hired those gents in the cabin to do two things: First they bushwhacked Travis Richmond and killed him while he was on his way to Garrison this morning. Then they rode into town and kidnapped Dolores. They had already brought Richmond's body here to the cabin, and they headed straight back here once they grabbed Dolores. Tompkins probably told them to put up a fight for a little while, just to make it look good, then to light a shuck out of here, leaving both Richmond and Dolores dead behind them. It's pure luck they hadn't gotten around to killing Dolores before Tompkins double-crossed them."

"I ain't never heard a crazier story," Tompkins growled. "You're makin' this up as you go along."

"I don't think so," Stark said. "You didn't intend for *anybody* to walk out of that cabin alive, Tompkins. That's why you brought your ranch hands over here and attacked the place like you did. If everybody in there had died, Richmond would have been blamed for what happened, and Dolores would be out of the way, too. How did you know Juan had left her the valley in his will?"

"Seemed like something the damned old coot would do—" Tompkins stopped short and cursed as Higgins drew the bandage tight around his wounded shoulder.

"So you didn't know for sure, but you were making certain anyway," Stark went on. "You wanted to put a stop to the land grant business, get your old enemy Richmond out of the way, and make yourself look like a hero all at the same time. Then, with Cord still in jail and likely to be convicted of murdering Juan, you could move in on Antlers and take it over. I hear tell you've had your eyes on this spread for a long time, Tompkins. With it under your control, you'd have practically the whole valley. Would've been just a matter of time before you squeezed out the smaller ranchers."

"Sounds like a plan Ben would come up with," Chadwick commented. "And it's the only reason I can think of that he would try to kill you like he did, Judge."

"Yep, I sort of fouled things up by getting in the cabin first and seeing the way Tompkins reacted." Stark faced the angry cattleman. "Tell me, did you hire that fella to break into my hotel room and steal the land grant documents?"

"Damn right I did," Tompkins shot back. "You didn't think I'd let some no-good drunken greaser take my land, did you?"

"You didn't think up the scheme to get rid of Richmond until later, I reckon." Stark shook his head in disgust and said to Sheriff Higgins, "Take him on back to town. You can hold him on charges of murder, attempted murder, and kidnapping, since he was responsible for all of this."

"Be glad to," Higgins said. He gestured to some of the posse members, who led Tompkins away toward the horses on the other side of the meadow.

Stark turned to face the Boxed BT riders, who were regarding him with a mixture of hostility and confusion. Their natural loyalty was to Ben Tompkins; they had been bred to the code of riding for the brand, no matter what. And yet they had all just witnessed ample proof of Tompkins's treachery. Some of their friends had died in the attack on the cabin, victims of their boss's convoluted plan.

The Diablo Grant

"I know you boys had no idea what was really going on here," Stark told them. "I'm not sure what'll happen to the Boxed BT now, but I know one thing—the ranch will still need somebody to take care of it. I reckon all of you ought to go home now."

For a tense moment the punchers did not respond. Then a couple of them nodded. "You're right, Judge," one said. "I reckon that's about all we can do for now." The others muttered agreement, and a few minutes later they had all gathered their horses, mounted up, and were riding back toward the other side of Diablo Valley.

"I'm glad they weren't stubborn about it," Chadwick said in a low voice. "They had the rest of us outnumbered."

Stark nodded. "I guess they realized Tompkins wasn't worth throwing away their lives for, after all."

At that moment, Matt Curry and Don Alfonso emerged from the cabin. Dolores, still pale and obviously shaken, walked unsteadily between them. Stark turned toward her and asked, "Are you all right?"

"*Sí*. I . . . I will be, Señor Stark. I still cannot believe I am not dead. Those men told me they had been paid to make sure that I died."

"Tompkins paid them," Stark told her, and Dolores nodded.

"*Sí*, that is what I think, too. They cursed him when they saw him and his men attacking the cabin. They said he was a double-crossing bastard."

That testimony was the last bit of proof Stark needed to support the theory he had pieced together. All the questions were answered now.

Or were they? Stark suddenly had the feeling that

185

he had overlooked something. Ben Tompkins was guilty of Travis Richmond's murder and the kidnapping of Dolores; there was no doubt of that, even though his hired guns had committed the actual crimes. But there was something else—

Before Stark could ponder it any longer, Dolores said pitifully, "I do not want this valley. Do I have to take it, Señor Stark? All it has brought to Juan and me is suffering."

Matt Curry looked crestfallen, no doubt realizing that, if not for his accidental discovery of the land grant papers, none of this would have happened. Stark wanted to tell the young man not to blame himself so much—Curry had had no choice but to come forward with his discovery—but at the moment he was more concerned with Dolores.

"Maybe the best thing for you to do would be to leave these parts," Stark told her gently. "There'll be plenty of money for you to start over anywhere you want. You can make a whole new life for yourself."

For the first time, he saw a flicker of hope in the young woman's eyes. "I would like to do this thing," she said softly.

"I'll help you make all the arrangements," Chadwick said. "And I'm sure Matt will be glad to help, too."

"You bet," Curry said eagerly. "I'm sorry for all this trouble, Dolores. I never meant for any of it to happen this way."

She took a deep breath and told him, "Do not blame yourself, Señor Curry. The workings of fate are . . . not for us to question."

Curry looked grateful for her understanding, and he and Don Alfonso led her away toward the horses. The

The Diablo Grant

posse was getting mounted up and ready to ride back to Garrison.

Stark and Chadwick followed them, and as he walked along beside the lawyer, Stark thought about what Dolores had said about the workings of fate. Maybe it didn't do any good to question such things.

But the things that *men* did, well, that was different.

And there were still some questions that Stark was going to see answered.

Chapter Fourteen

By the next day, the story of Travis Richmond's murder, Dolores's kidnapping, and Ben Tompkins's plot to get rid of both of them was all over Garrison. In addition, the townspeople had heard about Juan Espina's will leaving everything to Dolores, and the reaction was about what Stark had expected. Dolores was not going to be very popular around here, which made his suggestion that she leave this part of the territory and start a new life elsewhere even more appealing.

However, the ordeal the young woman had suffered at the hands of Tompkins's hired guns elicited some sympathy from the citizens, and Stark had a feeling no one would bother her while she remained in Garrison.

He met with her and Chadwick in her hotel room

The Diablo Grant

that afternoon. Dolores had regained some of her composure, but she was still somewhat shaken by the events of the day before. As she and Chadwick hashed out the details of where she wanted to go and what she wanted to do once she got there, Stark picked up a thick, leather-bound volume that was sitting on the dresser. He recognized it as the Bible in which Curry had found the land grant documents. As one of Juan's possessions, the Bible now belonged to Dolores.

Casually Stark turned to the pages in the back of the Bible on which the family history of the Espinas had been recorded through the years. He wondered again what had happened to the family to reduce it to the point that Juan was the only surviving member, but there were no answers to be found here, only names and dates inscribed in faded ink.

And yet there was a story here, Stark mused, if one looked beyond the names and dates. Births, marriages, deaths: It was a story common to all families. Common, yet different, if only in the details.

Stark's finger traced the lineage of the Espinas, pausing when he reached the final few entries. They were in Juan's familiar scrawl, the handwriting that some old padre at the mission had taught him. The deaths of Juan's parents were recorded here, as well as his marriage to a girl named Antonia, and the birth of their daughter.

Stark looked up abruptly and interrupted the conversation between Dolores and Chadwick. "Sorry to butt in," he said, "but what was your mother's name, Dolores?"

She frowned slightly as she replied, "Serafina. Why do you ask, Judge?"

"Do you remember much about her?"

"To my regret, no. She died when I was very young. I know only what I was told about her later, that she . . . that she was a prostitute, too. She died of one of the sicknesses that happen so often to such women."

"I'm sorry," Stark told her. "I didn't mean to bring up bad memories."

Dolores smiled faintly and shook her head. "My memories of my mother are not bad ones. I remember her voice and her soft touch and the warmth of her breath as she kissed me. No matter what else she did in her life, those are good memories."

"Yes," Stark agreed, "they are."

"What's this about, Judge?" Chadwick asked. "I reckon I know you well enough by now to know when you're on to something."

Stark tapped the Bible with a blunt finger. "I just noticed in here that Juan and his wife had a daughter named Serafina."

Dolores's eyes widened. "You mean—"

"Her name is the last entry in the family history," Stark said. "There's no record of her marriage or death, nor any record of grandchildren, either. But I reckon it's possible. Maybe Juan was ashamed of how his daughter turned out, especially after his wife died, but he still cared enough about her to list her here in the family Bible."

"And if I was his granddaughter—"

"Then he cared enough about you to keep track of you and protect you as best he could," Stark said. "I reckon he didn't put you down in the book because he never wanted *you* to know that your grandfather was the town drunk."

Tears welled up in Dolores's eyes and rolled down her cheeks. "All that time . . . all those years . . ."

Chadwick reached out and took her hand. "All that time he loved you, Dolores. That's what you ought to remember."

She nodded. "*Sí. Sí*, I will remember." Stark handed her the Bible, and she clutched it to her. "I will always remember."

"I reckon this strengthens your claim to the land grant," Stark told her. "Nobody's going to be able to break Juan's will or dispute your claim now."

Chadwick nodded in agreement. "The judge is right, Dolores. It really is all over now."

Well, not quite, Stark added silently. The matter of Dolores's heritage was settled, but that was all.

He asked one of the questions that was still nagging at him. "Dolores, Juan usually had some money, didn't he?"

She nodded again. "*Sí*. Never very much, but he always had a few coins."

"And I found that pouch full of coins in his shack," Stark pointed out.

"That's right," Chadwick said with a sudden frown. "We never did figure out who jumped you there, did we?"

"Nope. Tompkins was nowhere around and wouldn't have had any reason to knock me out and steal those coins and that little book." Stark looked at Dolores again. "Did you ever see Juan writing in a book about like this?" He indicated the size with his hands.

She shook her head, obviously baffled. "Never."

Stark grunted. "Juan was a man who liked to keep his secrets," he mused. "You didn't give him money, did you, Dolores?"

"No. I tried, but he would never accept it. In fact, there were times when he gave *me* money. I hated to take his coins, but sometimes I had to."

"I don't imagine he begrudged them," Stark assured her. He stood up and paced back and forth as his brain worked stubbornly at the puzzle of Juan Espina's life and death. "Juan was getting money from somewhere. Somebody knocked me out and stole that book from his shack. And Cord Richmond says that Juan was already dead when he got to the hotel. All that ought to add up to something."

"You think Cord was telling the truth?" Chadwick asked, his interest quickening.

"There are at least two loose ends we know of: Juan's money and whoever clouted me on the head. No reason why Juan's murder can't be another loose end—if we believe Cord's story."

"Tompkins could have killed Juan. He admitted he hired that drifter to break into your room and steal the land grant papers. He was willing to go to just about any lengths to make sure Juan didn't get his hands on Diablo Valley."

"It was already too late for that. I had already ruled in Juan's favor when he was killed. If Juan had been murdered *before* my ruling, I'd be more likely to accept Tompkins or one of his hired guns as the killer."

"The same line of reasoning works for Cord Richmond, though," Chadwick pointed out. "It was too late to stop the land grant from being upheld."

Stark nodded slowly and said, "But we never figured Cord killed Juan to stop the land grant. We thought Cord just got carried away and strangled Juan in the heat of the moment while they were arguing about what

The Diablo Grant

was going to happen to the ranchers up there. And we *know* Cord didn't hit me on the head, because he was locked up at the time."

"Well," Chadwick said, exasperation plain in his voice, "if Tompkins didn't do it, and Cord didn't do it, then who did—and why?"

Stark looked at the Bible Dolores was still holding and said, "I don't know yet. But maybe I've got an idea how to find out."

It was late in the afternoon when Stark found Matt Curry at the bank, just before closing. As Curry stood up from the chair in front of Edmund Wells's desk, where the two men had been talking, Stark hurried over and took hold of his arm. He gave Wells a cursory nod as he said, "Glad I was able to find you, Matt. There's been a new development in the Espina case."

"What?" Curry exclaimed. "I thought that was all over."

"So did I," Wells put in.

Stark shook his head. "I found something else inside Juan's old Bible. Did you know that the front flyleaf was pasted down?"

Curry's eyes widened in surprise. "I never thought to look for something like that. What was inside it?"

"Another document, folded up and sealed."

"What was it?" A note of anxiety had crept into Curry's voice.

Stark shook his head and said, "I don't know yet. I haven't opened it, and I don't plan to until I've got some witnesses. With everything that's happened so far, I'm not going to take the chance that somebody might think I tampered with the document, whatever it is."

"That's an excellent idea, Judge," Wells said. "This town—this whole part of the territory—has been in an uproar long enough. You need to put an end to this affair."

"Maybe this'll do it," Stark said. He looked at Curry again and went on, "Can you come back with me to my hotel room so that I can go ahead and open the thing?"

Curry grimaced. "I can't right now. I've got to meet Señorita Montoya. I promised to have an early supper with her."

Stark let out a grunt of impatience. "You mean to say courting some gal is more important to you than finding out what else Juan might've left behind?"

"Angelina's not just some gal," Curry said sheepishly. "I . . . I'm thinking about asking her to marry me."

Stark raised his eyebrows in surprise. "Didn't know that. Well, I reckon that's a good reason to keep your date, son. That paper's waited this long; I suppose it can wait another hour or so." Stark pointed a finger at Curry. "Not any longer than that, though."

"Sure, I'll be there. And I'll bring Mr. Chadwick along with me. He ought to be there, too."

Stark nodded. "Good idea. I'll see you both in an hour in my hotel room."

Curry hustled out of the bank, and Edmund Wells watched him go with a snort of displeasure. "Young people," he said scornfully. "When they get their heads full of romance, they don't think about anything else."

Stark had to grin. "Yeah, but it gives 'em something to remember when they get to be old geezers like us, eh, Mr. Wells?"

The Diablo Grant

The banker frowned at him haughtily, and Stark gave the man a casual wave as he left the building. He headed back toward the hotel, walking leisurely. As he moved along the boardwalk he looked around Garrison, looked at the townspeople and the buildings, and thought, not for the first time, that it was a pretty nice community as cattle towns went. From what he had seen of Diablo Valley, it lived up to its reputation as one of the best areas for ranching in New Mexico Territory. He had instinctively liked Travis Richmond, and he felt there might be some good in Cord Richmond, too, buried under that impulsive streak.

None of them had deserved the trouble that had befallen them, Stark mused. Not Richmond and his son, not the citizens of Garrison, and certainly not Juan Espina and Dolores. But like a house of cards, once things started to fall, they had to continue to the inevitable end.

There were only a few cards left standing, Stark knew, and they were teetering precariously.

When he reached the hotel, he went straight up to his room and shut the door, then took off his hat and coat and sat down on the bed. There was nothing to do now but wait.

Stark didn't have to wait long.

Less than a quarter of an hour had passed when a brisk knock sounded on the door. Stark stood up and went over to answer it. When he swung the door open, he wasn't surprised to see Edmund Wells standing in the corridor. The banker had put on his hat, and he had a solemn expression on his florid face.

"Hello again, Your Honor," Wells said. "Could I come in for a moment?"

"Sure," Stark said as he stepped back to let Wells into the room. He shut the door again and turned to face him. "What can I do for you?"

"Actually, I thought perhaps I could do something for you," Wells said. "After you left the bank, it occurred to me that I might be able to serve as the witness you need when you open that document you found in Juan Espina's Bible."

Stark frowned. "I'm waiting for Matt Curry and Billy Chadwick. They'll be here in a little while."

"Yes, I'm aware of that, but you seemed rather disappointed when young Curry refused to break his, ah, dinner engagement with that Mexican woman. There's really no point in waiting. Anyone in this part of the country will tell you that I'm one of the territory's most reputable citizens. I can swear that no one tampered with the document, and that will carry just as much weight as the word of Curry and Chadwick."

Stark appeared to think that over for a moment, but then he shook his head. "No, I reckon I'd better wait," he said. "But you're welcome to stay around and see what the thing says once I open it up. Like you said, you're an important man, and I'd be glad for the extra witness."

"I can't convince you to go ahead and—"

"Nope," Stark cut in flatly.

Wells laughed nervously. "Well, I suppose I was being a bit impatient. I'm as curious as anyone, you know. I can't for the life of me figure out what else that old man might have had hidden."

His voice taking on a confidential tone, Stark said, "I think it must have something to do with the way

The Diablo Grant

Juan always had a little money on hand. He was getting those coins from somewhere—or *somebody*."

That did it, finally. Stark was beginning to wonder if anything was going to prod Wells into losing his head. But as Stark spoke, the banker's face twisted, and he stepped back suddenly, reaching under his coat with surprising speed. He brought out a small pistol and pointed it at Stark.

"Don't move, Judge," he said sharply. "I want that document, and I want it now. Hand it over or I'll kill you."

Stark regarded him with a cold, hard stare. "What's the matter, Wells? You afraid Juan made more than one copy of that information he was using to blackmail you?"

Wells's eyes narrowed slightly, as if he were trying to guess exactly how much Stark had figured out. "Just give me the paper," he grated.

Stark ignored the demand. "You must've figured you were safe after you knocked me out in Juan's shack and stole that journal of his. You took the coins, too, just to confuse the issue, but what you were really after was that little book."

"He was a filthy old man!" Wells said viciously. "He had no right to even talk to me, let alone to extort money from me!"

"You had to pay, though, didn't you? After all, you're probably Garrison's most prominent citizen—banker, mayor, civic leader, deacon in the local church. I've been asking around about you, Wells. A man like you couldn't afford to have Juan telling everybody what you'd been up to."

"It was only a few times, damn it! The girls were well paid." Wells's voice turned into a whine. "A man has needs, you know, even a man like me."

Stark had figured it was something like that. "So Juan saw you sneaking around the red-light district, maybe even saw you coming out of some girl's crib. He knew what that knowledge could mean for him. But he wasn't ambitious. The tequila had burned any ambition out of him. All he wanted from you was a few coins whenever he needed them to buy a bottle or give to Dolores. And you were more than willing to pay him to keep your secret."

The pistol shook slightly in Wells's hand. "You're just stalling for time," he accused. "It's not going to work. I'm going to get that document, and then—"

"And then what?" Stark cut in. "You plan on killing me, too, like you killed Juan? Everything changed when this land grant business came up. All those visions of wealth and power went to Juan's head, and he planned to get back at everybody who had ever looked down on him, including you, Wells. What better way for Juan to even the score than to reveal what he knew about you?"

Wells's face was pale except for two red splotches that stood out on his cheeks. "He wasn't just a cheap blackmailer anymore," he said. "He wasn't interested in money, just in destroying things . . . destroying people. I had to stop him."

"Which you did by choking him to death in the room across the hall."

Wells jerked his head in a nod. "What gave me away?"

"Only a few people knew I was going out to Juan's

The Diablo Grant

shack that day to look through his things. Billy Chadwick was one of them. But I told him about it when I ran into him in the bank. *You* were there, too, Wells, and you were the only one with enough to lose that you were willing to attack me. Juan probably told you a long time ago that he had written down everything he knew about you, just as a precaution. You couldn't take a chance on my finding anything, and when you came in and saw me with that book and the pouch of coins in my hand, you knew you had to get them away from me." Stark lifted a hand to his head and touched the spot where Wells had hit him. It was still tender. "I don't like being pistol-whipped, mister."

The banker's features stiffened into self-righteous lines. "I couldn't allow those things to get out. I wasn't the only one Espina was blackmailing, you know. Nobody paid any attention to a miserable drunk, so he saw a lot of things in this town that he shouldn't have." His voice shook with indignation as he went on, "I did this entire community a service by killing that filthy old man and then burning that book you found."

"You didn't do old Juan a favor, though, did you?" Stark's words lashed at Wells. "Or Cord Richmond, either. Did you intend to let him hang to cover your tracks, Wells?"

"If necessary. And you, unfortunately, Judge, are going to be killed by a robber you surprised in your hotel room—as soon as you hand over that document, that is."

The door opened and Billy Chadwick said, "I don't think so."

Wells jerked toward the unexpected interruption, and

Stark lunged at him. The judge's left hand lashed out, batting the little pistol aside as it cracked wickedly. The next instant, Stark's right fist crashed into Wells's jaw with all the power of his burly form behind it. Wells was driven backward by the punch and fell over the bed, the gun slipping from his fingers as he rolled off onto the floor.

By that time Sheriff Higgins was in the room, too, and he loomed over Wells and trained his own revolver on the banker. "I reckon you better not move, Mayor," Higgins said gloomily. "I'd hate like hell to have to shoot you, even after all that stuff we heard from out there in the hall."

Matt Curry had followed Chadwick and Higgins into the room, and the young editor looked at Stark in amazement as the judge rubbed the bruised knuckles of his right hand. "You were right, Your Honor," Curry said. "You had the whole thing figured out, and Mr. Wells took the bait just like you said he would. He figured that document you invented really existed."

"Well, I was a mite lucky," Stark said. "All the pieces fit together, as best I could tell, but you never know when some wild card will show up. This time it didn't."

"But how did you do it?" Curry asked. "How did you figure it out?"

Stark looked at the young journalist with a mixture of regret and amusement. "Another story for your paper, Matt?"

"Well . . ."

Stark waved his hand. "Never mind. I reckon folks have a right to know. You heard what I told Wells about how I knew he was the only one who could've jumped me at Juan's shack. I figured there had to be some-

The Diablo Grant

thing like blackmail behind everything, because even the most upstanding folks have things they don't want anybody else to know about. In my line of work, you get to hear a lot of dirty little secrets." He sighed wearily. "Too many secrets, most of the time."

Sheriff Higgins pulled Wells to his feet and marched the crestfallen banker out of the room.

As Chadwick watched them go, he shook his head sadly. "I hate to see something like this happen. Edmund Wells wasn't really a bad man. At least he didn't start out that way."

"No, I agree with you," Stark said. "But that doesn't excuse murder. Juan Espina didn't deserve to die, and Wells would have let Cord Richmond hang for the crime."

"I guess Cord will go free now, since we all heard Wells confess. But his father's still dead."

Stark nodded. The old king of Spain had had no inkling what a bloody string of events he was spawning when he granted Diablo Valley to the Espina family.

But life was like that, Stark supposed, good and bad both spreading out like ripples in a pond, rolling on down through the ages, and the outcome was always impossible to predict. All a man could do was wait and see where the ripples would take him next . . . and try not to let them pull him under.

Chapter Fifteen

Cord Richmond was holding up pretty well considering all he had been through, Stark observed a couple of days later as he watched the young man signing the papers that Billy Chadwick had drawn up. Cord looked drawn and haggard, but there was a new maturity and determination in his eyes. He was going to take over the running of Antlers and continue the Richmond tradition. Stark had a hunch Travis Richmond would have been proud of his son.

Chadwick's office was rather crowded at the moment. Stark was there, of course, and so were Cord and Dolores, completing the transaction that returned Diablo Valley to the control of the cattlemen who had been there for years. Dolores was selling the valley outright, rather than leasing it to the ranchers, but her

The Diablo Grant

price was extremely reasonable, and the deal Chadwick had arranged allowed Cord and the other cattlemen to pay off their debt over a long period of time. Dolores would have plenty of money to make the fresh start in life she wanted, and Cord Richmond and his fellow ranchers wouldn't have to break themselves to hang on to their land. It just went to show that most things could be worked out if folks would let themselves be reasonable.

But all too often, Stark mused, being reasonable wasn't something most people could manage.

Cord was buying the Boxed BT, too, since Ben Tompkins was in jail awaiting trial on murder charges along with Edmund Wells. The ranch would be absorbed into Antlers, making the Richmond spread one of the largest in the entire territory. Running it was going to be one hell of a job, but Stark had a feeling Cord would be up to the task.

Matt Curry was here in the lawyer's office, too; the signing of these contracts was definitely newsworthy. Standing beside him was Angelina Montoya. Her father, Don Alfonso, looked on with an expression of satisfaction as Cord and Dolores finalized the deal. Only when Don Alfonso glanced toward his daughter and Matt Curry did he look like any typical worried father. To the surprise of everyone except Matt and Angelina, the young newspaperman had gone through with what he had told Stark he wanted to do: He had asked Angelina to marry him.

And she had said yes.

"Well, that's that," Chadwick said as he gathered up the papers Cord and Dolores had signed.

"Good," Cord said. He stood up. "I've got to get back to the ranch. It's going to be mighty busy out there for a while, I reckon." He summoned up a smile and extended a hand to Dolores. "Good luck to you, señorita."

She hesitated, obviously not accustomed to such a respectful tone from the young man. But then she returned his smile and took his hand briefly. *"Gracias,"* she murmured. "I wish you much luck with Diablo Valley, señor."

Cord's smile widened into a grin. "Come back and see it again someday," he said. "I've got a hunch you'll like the way it turns out."

"So do I," Stark said. He shook hands with Cord and went on, "Sorry about your dad and everything else that happened."

A flicker of grief went through Cord's eyes. "You were just doing your job, Judge. Reckon I understand that now. I've got a job of my own to do, though, so I'd better get after it." He put on his hat, said his good-byes to the others, and clattered down the stairs outside.

Don Alfonso turned his stern expression on Matt Curry and said, "You and I must go and have a talk, young man. We have much to discuss."

Angelina took Matt's arm. "If there is any talking to be done, I will be there, too," she insisted.

Her father frowned at her. "I suppose there is no chance of persuading you to act like a proper young lady and obey your elders?"

"None at all," Angelina said with a laugh.

"Very well. Come with me, both of you." Montoya

The Diablo Grant

looked at the young editor. "I am afraid you do not know what you are getting into, Matthew."

"I'm willing to find out," Matt said as the three of them started down the stairs.

Dolores stood up. "I must go, too. The stagecoach for Santa Fe will be here soon. I will let you know where to send my money, Señor Chadwick."

"You do that, Dolores," the lawyer told her. "And don't worry about a thing. I'll take care of all of it for you."

"*Sí*, I trust you." She looked at Stark. "And you, señor. I can only thank you for everything—"

"No thanks necessary," Stark said gruffly. "The United States government pays me to sort out these things, and that's what I do. It's all part of the job."

Dolores came up on her tiptoes and brushed her lips across his bearded cheek. "I will say *gracias* anyway. For myself, and for my grandfather."

"Both of you are welcome," Stark told her gently.

When Dolores was gone, Chadwick looked at Stark and said, "Well, I reckon that just leaves us."

"A couple of old warhorses," Stark agreed.

Chadwick raised an eyebrow. "Thirsty warhorses?" he asked with a grin. He reached into the bottom drawer of his desk and brought out a bottle of whiskey. "This is the real thing, not some homemade panther piss."

Stark nodded. "Sounds like a mighty good idea."

As Chadwick took out a couple of glasses and poured the whiskey, he asked, "What are you going to do now, Judge?"

"What I always do: wire my bosses in Washington and let 'em know this case is over. I reckon they've got something else lined up for me by now, some sort of mess that needs untangling. They usually do."

Chadwick grinned. "You going to untangle it with brains or bullets, Your Honor?"

"Whatever it takes, Counselor, whatever it takes. And one more thing: Seeing as you're a fellow Texan and all, from here on out, call me Big Earl."

Epilogue

"... call me Big Earl," the old man said.

When there was no response, he looked down and saw that the boy was sound asleep in the chair beside him. The old man smiled and carefully slipped his arms around the little form so that he could stand up. The boy was getting pretty heavy, he thought, but the old man carried him effortlessly up the stairs and slipped him into bed, right under the pictures of Buck Jones and Tom Mix that the boy had cut off cereal boxes and thumbtacked to the wall.

As he came down the stairs, the old man heard his grandson and his grandson's wife coming in the front door. They were laughing happily, and the old man was glad they had enjoyed their evening out at the picture show. He certainly hadn't minded watching his great-grandson, even if the little scudder *had* dozed off on him before he finished the story of the Diablo Valley land grant. Not enough action, he supposed, and anyway, real life was never quite as clear-cut and dramatic as those yarns they printed in the pulps.

"Any problems, Gramps?" his grandson asked as the old man reached the bottom of the stairs.

"Nope. The little un's asleep. Just took him up and put him to bed."

"You didn't fill his head with a lot of wild stories about the old days, did you?" asked the boy's mother, drawing a quick glance of disapproval from her husband.

"'Course not," the old man said. "I just told him a little about how it really was."

He pretended not to see the way she rolled her eyes as she turned away.

"Sorry, Gramps," the young man said quietly as his wife went into the kitchen. "She doesn't really understand."

The old man clapped a hand on his grandson's shoulder. "Don't you worry about it. I know old codgers like me sometimes talk a mite too much. What picture'd you see tonight?"

"The new William S. Hart. It's called *Tumbleweeds*. I think you'd like it, Gramps. It's about the Oklahoma land rush."

"Well, maybe I'll go see it one of these days," the old man said. "I was there for the land rush, you know. Never have quite gotten used to the idea of moving pictures, though."

"They say they'll be talking in another few years."

The old man shook his head. "Moving *and* talking pictures? Don't seem right to me."

The Diablo Grant

They both fell silent as the young man's wife moved past them again and went up the stairs. The young man looked after her and said, "Well, good night, Gramps. Don't stay up too late working on your memoirs."

"I'll try not to. You sure my pecking on that typewriter doesn't bother you?"

"Not at all," the young man said. "You go right ahead. I'm glad to see somebody getting some use out of the thing."

He went up the stairs with the seemingly boundless energy of the young. The old man shook his head and turned toward the small table tucked into a corner of the living room. A typewriter sat there, with a stack of blank paper beside it. The old man worked there nearly every night after his grandson's family had gone to bed, but he never left any typed pages lying around for them to find the next day. Those went up in his own room, locked away until he was done and ready to mail them off to New York. His family thought he was working on his memoirs, a dusty set of recollections that would never be published. But what they didn't know wouldn't hurt 'em, the old man thought. That was why he had decided to use a pen name.

He pulled back the chair and settled his still powerful frame into it. He was mighty glad he had hit on this idea. Along with his government pension, the money his work brought in was enough to make life comfortable for all of them, and they had been able to save some, too. Things were booming along right now, but they might not always be that way. The old man had seen enough life to know that after every boom nearly always came a bust.

With a frown of concentration, he pulled on his short

white beard and tried to decide what to write next. There was no shortage of yarns in his head; after all, he had been on the federal bench out there in the Southwestern District for a whole heap of years. It was simply a matter of figuring out which one to tell next—dressed up a little, of course, because his readers *did* like their blood and thunder.

Abruptly the old man smiled and nodded. He would tell the story of the talkative little half-breed girl called Mockingbird and how she'd nearly gotten both of them killed a time or two, not to mention how the whole business had damn near disrupted the entire United States government and almost started a war. That was a good 'un, the old man thought.

He typed: *Big Earl Plays the Long Odds, by John B. Boothe.*

About the Author

Judge Earl Stark is the latest creation of veteran author James Reasoner, who has written over seventy novels, including westerns, mysteries, and historical sagas. A lifelong Texan and a member of the Western Writers of America, Reasoner has worked as a newspaper columnist and bookstore manager in addition to his fiction writing. He is an avid reader and tries to write the sort of books he enjoys reading. Reasoner and his wife Livia (who also writes novels, under the name L.J. Washburn) live in the Texas countryside with their two daughters, Shayna and Joanna, and an assortment of dogs, cats, ducks, and Nigerian dwarf goats. He hopes to someday have a better fence.

THE BEST WESTERN NOVELS COME FROM POCKET BOOKS

Sam Brown
- ☐ THE CRIME OF COY BELL.................78543-5/$3.99
- ☐ THE LONG SEASON.......67186-3/$4.50

Robert J. Conley
- ☐ GO-AHEAD RIDER.........74365-1/$3.50
- ☐ BORDER LINE..............74931-5/$3.50
- ☐ CRAZY SNAKE..............77902-8/$4.99
- ☐ NED CHRISTIE'S WAR....75969-8/$3.99
- ☐ GERONIMO: AN AMERICAN LEGEND....88982-6/$5.50
- ☐ ZEKE PROCTOR: CHEROKEE OUTLAW: ...77901-X/$4.99

Jack Curtis
- ☐ CUT AND BRANDED......79321-7/$3.99
- ☐ THE QUIET COWBOY...79317-9/$3.99
- ☐ THE MARK OF CAIN....79316-0/$3.99

James M. Reasoner
- ☐ STARK'S JUSTICE..........87140-4/$3.99
- ☐ THE HAWTHORNE LEGACY ....87141-2/$4.99
- ☐ THE DIABLO GRANT....87142-0/$4.99

Dusty Richards
- ☐ FROM HELL TO BREAKFAST ....87241-9/$3.99

R.C. House
- ☐ VERDICT AT MEDICINE SPRINGS..................87244-3/$4.99
- ☐ REQUIEM FOR A RUSTLER..................76043-2/$3.99
- ☐ RYERSON'S MANHUNT..................87243-5/$3.99

Jim Miller
THE EX-RANGERS
- ☐ #9: CARSTON'S LAW.....74827-0/$3.50
- ☐ #10:STRANGER FROM NOWHERE..................74828-9/$3.99
- ☐ #11: SOUTH OF THE BORDER..................74829-7/$3.99

Giles Tippette
- ☐ THE BUTTON HORSE...79347-0/$4.50
- ☐ THE HORSE THIEVES...79345-4/$3.99
- ☐ SLICK MONEY..............79346-2/$4.50
- ☐ MEXICAN STANDOFF...87158-7/$4.99
- ☐ THE DUEL..................87159-5/$4.99

Bruce H. Thorstad
- ☐ THE TIMES OF WICHITA..................70657-8/$3.50
- ☐ THE GENTS.................75904-3/$4.50
- ☐ SHARPSHOOTERS....75906-X/$3.99
- ☐ ACE OF DIAMONDS...88583-9/$3.99

Barton & Williams
- ☐ SHADOW OF DOUBT.....74578-6/$4.50

Simon & Schuster Mail Order
200 Old Tappan Rd., Old Tappan, N.J. 07675
Please send me the books I have checked above. I am enclosing $_____ (please add $0.75 to cover the postage and handling for each order. Please add appropriate sales tax). Send check or money order–no cash or C.O.D.'s please. Allow up to six weeks for delivery. For purchase over $10.00 you may use VISA: card number, expiration date and customer signature must be included.

Name _____
Address _____
City _____ State/Zip _____
VISA Card # _____ Exp.Date _____
Signature _____

728-08

The *only* authorized biography of the legendary man who inspired two of the year's biggest movie events!

WYATT ☆ EARP
FRONTIER MARSHAL

"No man could have a more loyal friend than Wyatt Earp might be, nor a more dangerous enemy."
— Bat Masterson

"Earp never hunted trouble, but he was ready for any that came his way." —Jimmy Cairns, deputy marshal, Wichita, Kansas

"I am not ashamed of anything I ever did." — Wyatt Earp

Available in paperback from Pocket Books